Homer

Odysseus Returns Home

TRANSLATED BY ROBERT FAGLES

PENGUIN EPICS

PENGUIN BOOKS

Published by the Penguin Group
Penguin Books Ltd, 80 Strand, London WC2R ORL, England
Penguin Group (USA) Inc., 375 Hudson Street, New York, New York 10014, USA
Penguin Group (Canada), 90 Eglinton Avenue East, Suite 700, Toronto, Ontario, Canada M4P 2Y3
(a division of Pearson Penguin Canada Inc.)
Penguin Ireland, 25 St Stephen's Green, Dublin 2, Ireland (a division of Penguin Books Ltd)
Penguin Group (Australia), 250 Camberwell Road, Camberwell, Victoria 3124, Australia
(a division of Pearson Australia Group Pty Ltd)
Penguin Books India Pvt Ltd, 11 Community Centre, Panchsheel Park, New Delhi – 110 017, India
Penguin Group (NZ), cnr Airborne and Rosedale Roads, Albany,
Auckland 1310, New Zealand (a division of Pearson New Zealand Ltd)
Penguin Books (South Africa) (Pty) Ltd, 24 Sturdee Avenue,
Rosebank, Johannesburg 2196, South Africa

Penguin Books Ltd, Registered Offices: 80 Strand, London WC2R ORL, England

www.penguin.com

This translation of *The Odyssey* first published in the United States of America
by Viking Penguin 1996
First published in Penguin Books 1997
This extract published in Penguin Books 2006

1

Translation copyright © Robert Fagles, 1996
All rights reserved

The moral right of the translator has been asserted

Taken from the Penguin Classics edition of *The Odyssey*, translated by Robert Fagles

Typeset by Rowland Phototypesetting Ltd, Bury St Edmunds, Suffolk
Printed in England by Clays Ltd, St Ives plc

ISBN-13: 978-0-141-02629-9
ISBN-10: 0-141-02629-4

Contents

Note

This extract from Homer's *The Odyssey* picks up at the point where the wily hero Odysseus returns to his home, Ithaca, following his long journey back from the Trojan War. But he returns to find his wife, Penelope, besieged by a host of aggressive suitors who are led by the boorish Antinous. So, with the help of his son Telemachus, Odysseus returns to his palace disguised as a beggar with a plan to overcome them.

I

The Beggar-King of Ithaca

Now along came this tramp, this public nuisance
who used to scrounge a living round the streets of Ithaca –
notorious for his belly, a ravenous, bottomless pit
for food and drink, but he had no pith, no brawn,
despite the looming hulk that met your eyes.
Arnaeus was his name,
so his worthy mother called him at birth,
but all the young men called him Irus for short
because he'd hustle messages at any beck and call.
Well *he* came by to rout the king from his own house
and met Odysseus now with a rough, abusive burst:
'Get off the porch, you old goat, before I haul you
off by the leg! Can't you see them give me the wink,
all of them here, to drag you out – and so I would
but I've got some pangs of conscience. Up with you, man,
or before you know it, we'll be trading blows!'

                                     A killing look,
and the wily old soldier countered, 'Out of your mind?
What damage have I done *you*? What have I said?
I don't grudge you anything,
not if the next man up and gives you plenty.
This doorsill is big enough for the both of us –
You've got no call to grudge me what's not yours.
You're another vagrant, just like me, I'd say,
and it lies with the gods to make us rich or poor. So,

I

keep your fists to yourself, don't press your luck, don't rile
    me,
or old as I am, I'll bloody your lip, splatter your chest
and buy myself some peace and quiet for tomorrow.
I doubt you'll ever come lumbering back again
to the halls of Laertes' royal son Odysseus.'

    'Look who's talking!' the beggar rumbled in anger.
'How this pot-bellied pig runs off at the mouth –
like an old crone at her oven!
Well *I*'ve got a knock-out blow in store for *him* –
I'll batter the tramp with both fists, crack every tooth
from his jaws, I'll litter the ground with teeth
like a rogue sow's, punished for rooting corn!
Belt up – so the lords can see us fight it out.
How can you beat a champion half your age?'

    Tongue-lashing each other, tempers flaring,
there on the polished sill before the lofty doors.
And Antinous, that grand prince, hearing them wrangle,
broke into gloating laughter, calling out to the suitors,
'Friends, nothing like this has come our way before –
what sport some god has brought the palace now!
The stranger and Irus, look,
they'd battle it out together, fists flying.
Come, let's pit them against each other – fast!'

    All leapt from their seats with whoops of laughter,
clustering round the pair of ragged beggars there
as Eupithes' son Antinous planned the contest.
'Quiet, my fine friends. Here's what I propose.

These goat sausages sizzling here in the fire –
we packed them with fat and blood to have for supper.
Now, whoever wins this bout and proves the stronger,
let that man step up and take his pick of the lot!
What's more, from this day on he feasts among us –
no other beggar will we allow inside
to cadge his meals from us!'

                                    They all cheered
but Odysseus, foxy veteran, plotted on . . .
'Friends, how can an old man, worn down with pain,
stand up to a young buck? It's just this belly of mine,
this trouble-maker, tempts me to take a licking.
So first, all of you swear me a binding oath:
come, not one of you steps in for Irus here,
strikes me a foul blow to pull him through
and lays me in the dust.'

                                    And at that
they all mouthed the oath that he required,
and once they vowed they'd never interfere,
Prince Telemachus drove the matter home:
'Stranger, if your spine and fighting pride
prompt you to go against this fellow now,
have no fear of any suitor in the pack –
whoever fouls you will have to face a crowd.
Count on *me*, your host. And two lords back me up,
Antinous and Eurymachus – both are men of sense.'

   They all shouted approval of the prince
as Odysseus belted up, roping his rags around his loins,
baring his big rippling thighs – his boxer's broad shoulders,
his massive chest and burly arms on full display

as Athena stood beside him,
fleshing out the limbs of the great commander . . .
Despite their swagger, the suitors were amazed,
gaping at one another, trading forecasts:
'Irus will soon be ironed out for good!'

'He's in for the beating he begged for all along.'

'Look at the hams on that old-timer –'
                                        'Just under his rags!'

Each outcry jolted Irus to the core – too late.
The servants trussed his clothes up, dragged him on,
the flesh on his body quaking now with terror.
Antinous rounded on him, flinging insults:
'You, you clumsy ox, you're better off dead
or never born at all, if you cringe at *him*,
paralyzed with fear of an old, broken hulk,
ground down by the pains that hound his steps.
Mark my word – so help me I'll make it good –
if that old relic whips you and wins the day,
I'll toss you into a black ship and sail you off
to Echetus, the mainland king who wrecks all men alive!
He'll lop your nose and ears with his ruthless blade,
he'll rip your privates out by the roots, he will,
and serve them up to his dogs to bolt down raw!'

That threat shook his knees with a stronger fit
but they hauled him into the ring. Both men put up their
      fists –
with the seasoned fighter Odysseus deeply torn now . . .

should he knock him senseless, leave him dead where he
>   dropped
or just stretch him out on the ground with a light jab?
As he mulled things over, that way seemed the best:
a glancing blow, the suitors would not detect him.
The two men squared off –
>   and Irus hurled a fist
at Odysseus' right shoulder as *he* came through
with a hook below the ear, pounding Irus' neck,
smashing the bones inside –
>   suddenly red blood
came spurting out of his mouth, and headlong down
he pitched in the dust, howling, teeth locked in a grin,
feet beating the ground –
>   and the princely suitors,
flinging their hands in the air, died laughing.
Grabbing him by the leg, Odysseus hauled him
through the porch, across the yard to the outer gate,
heaped him against the courtyard wall, sitting slumped,
stuck his stick in his hand and gave him a parting shot:
'Now hold your post – play the scarecrow to all the pigs and
>   dogs!
But no more lording it over strangers, no more playing
the beggar-king for you, you loathsome fool,
or you'll bring down something worse around your
>   neck!'

  He threw his beggar's sack across his shoulders –
torn and tattered, slung from a fraying rope –
then back he went to the sill and took his seat.
The suitors ambled back as well, laughing jauntily,

toasting the beggar warmly now, those proud young blades,
one man egging the other on: 'Stranger, friend, may Zeus
and the other deathless gods fill up your sack with blessings!'

'All your heart desires!'
                         'You've knocked him out of action,
that insatiable tramp –'
                    'That parasite on the land!'

'Ship him off to Echetus, fast – the mainland king
who wrecks all men alive!'
                    Welcome words
and a lucky omen too – Odysseus' heart leapt up.
Antinous laid before him a generous goat sausage,
bubbling fat and blood. Amphinomus took two loaves
from the wicker tray and set them down beside him,
drank his health in a golden cup and said,
'Cheers, old friend, old father,
saddled now as you are with so much trouble –
here's to your luck, great days from this day on!'

And the one who knew the world replied at length,
'Amphinomus, you seem like a man of good sense to me.
Just like your father – at least I've heard his praises,
Nisus of Dulichion, a righteous man, and rich.
You're his son, they say, you seem well-spoken, too.
So I will tell you something. Listen. Listen closely.
Of all that breathes and crawls across the earth,
our mother earth breeds nothing feebler than a man.
So long as the gods grant him power, spring in his knees,
he thinks he will never suffer affliction down the years.

6

But then, when the happy gods bring on the long hard times,
bear them he must, against his will, and steel his heart.
Our lives, our mood and mind as we pass across the earth,
turn as the days turn . . .
as the father of men and gods makes each day dawn.
I too seemed destined to be a man of fortune once
and a wild wicked swath I cut, indulged my lust for violence,
staking all on my father and my brothers.

                                          Look at me now.
And so, I say, let no man ever be lawless all his life,
just take in peace what gifts the gods will send.

                                                        True,
but here I see you suitors plotting your reckless work,
carving away at the wealth, affronting the loyal wife
of a man who won't be gone from kin and country long.
I say he's right at hand – and may some power save you,
spirit you home before you meet him face-to-face
the moment he returns to native ground!
Once under his own roof, he and your friends,
believe you me, won't part till blood has flowed.'

                                                         With that
he poured out honeyed wine to the gods and drank deeply,
then restored the cup to the young prince's hands.
Amphinomus made his way back through the hall,
his heart sick with anguish, shaking his head,
fraught with grave foreboding . . .
but not even so could he escape his fate.
Even then Athena had bound him fast to death
at the hands of Prince Telemachus and his spear.
Now back he went to the seat that he'd left empty.

But now the goddess Athena with her glinting eyes
inspired Penelope, Icarius' daughter, wary, poised,
to display herself to her suitors, fan their hearts,
inflame them more, and make her even more esteemed
by her husband and her son than she had been before.
Forcing a laugh, she called her maid: 'Eurynome,
my spirit longs – though it never did till now –
to appear before my suitors, loathe them as I do.
I'd say a word to my son too, for his own good,
not to mix so much with that pernicious crowd,
so glib with their friendly talk
but plotting wicked plots they'll hatch tomorrow.'

'Well said, my child,' the old woman answered,
'all to the point. Go to the boy and warn him now,
hold nothing back. But first you should bathe yourself,
give a gloss to your face. Don't go down like that –
your eyes dimmed, your cheeks streaked with tears.
It makes things worse, this grieving on and on.
Your son's now come of age – your fondest prayer
to the deathless gods, to see him wear a beard.'

'Eurynome,' discreet Penelope objected,
'don't try to coax me, care for me as you do,
to bathe myself, refresh my face with oils.
Whatever glow I had died long ago . . .
the gods of Olympus snuffed it out that day
my husband sailed away in the hollow ships.
But please, have Autonoë and Hippodameia come
and support me in the hall. I'll never brave
those men alone. I'd be too embarrassed.'

Now as the old nurse bustled through the house
to give the women orders, call them to the queen,
the bright-eyed goddess thought of one more thing.
She drifted a sound slumber over Icarius' daughter,
back she sank and slept, her limbs fell limp and still,
reclining there on her couch, all the while Athena,
luminous goddess, lavished immortal gifts on her
to make her suitors lose themselves in wonder . . .
The divine unguent first. She cleansed her cheeks,
her brow and fine eyes with ambrosia smooth as the oils
the goddess Love applies, donning her crown of flowers
whenever she joins the Graces' captivating dances.
She made her taller, fuller in form to all men's eyes,
her skin whiter than ivory freshly carved, and now,
Athena's mission accomplished, off the bright one went
as bare-armed maids came in from their own quarters,
chattering all the way, and sleep released the queen.
She woke, touched her cheek with a hand, and mused,
'Ah, what a marvelous gentle sleep, enfolding me
in the midst of all my anguish! Now if only
blessed Artemis sent me a death as gentle, now,
this instant – no more wasting away my life,
my heart broken in longing for my husband . . .
He had every strength,
rising over his countrymen, head and shoulders.'

Then, leaving her well-lit chamber, she descended,
not alone: two of her women followed close behind.
That radiant woman, once she reached her suitors,
drawing her glistening veil across her cheeks,
paused now where a column propped the sturdy roof,

with one of her loyal handmaids stationed either side.
The suitors' knees went slack, their hearts dissolved in lust –
all of them lifted prayers to lie beside her, share her bed.
But turning toward her son, she warned, 'Telemachus,
your sense of balance is not what it used to be.
When you were a boy you had much better judgment.
Now that you've grown and reached your young prime
and any stranger, seeing how tall and handsome you are,
would think you the son of some great man of wealth –
now your sense of fairness seems to fail you.
Consider the dreadful thing just done in our halls –
how you let the stranger be so abused! Why,
suppose our guest, sitting here at peace,
here in our own house,
were hauled and badly hurt by such cruel treatment?
You'd be shamed, disgraced in all men's eyes!'

'Mother . . .' Telemachus paused, then answered.
'I cannot fault your anger at all this.
My heart takes note of everything, feels it, too,
both the good and the bad – the boy you knew is gone.
But how can I plan my world in a sane, thoughtful way?
These men drive me mad, hedging me round, right and left,
plotting their lethal plots, and no one takes my side.
Still, this battle between the stranger and Irus
hardly went as the suitors might have hoped:
the stranger beat him down!
If only – Father Zeus, Athena and lord Apollo –
these gallants, now, this moment, here in our house,
were battered senseless, heads lolling, knees unstrung,

some sprawled in the courtyard, some sprawled outside!
Slumped like Irus down at the front gates now,
whipped, and his head rolling like some drunk.
He can't stand up on his feet and stagger home,
whatever home he's got – the man's demolished.'

So Penelope and her son exchanged their hopes
as Eurymachus stepped in to praise the queen.
'Ah, daughter of Icarius, wise Penelope,
if all the princes in Ionian Argos saw you now!
What a troop of suitors would banquet in your halls
tomorrow at sunrise! You surpass all women
in build and beauty, refined and steady mind.'

'Oh no, Eurymachus,' wise Penelope demurred,
'whatever form and feature I had, what praise I'd won,
the deathless gods destroyed that day the Achaeans
sailed away to Troy, my husband in their ships,
Odysseus – if *he* could return to tend my life
the renown I had would only grow in glory.
Now my life is torment . . .
look at the griefs some god has loosed against me!
I'll never forget the day he left this land of ours;
he caught my right hand by the wrist and said, gently,
'Dear woman, I doubt that every Achaean under arms
will make it home from Troy, all safe and sound.
The Trojans, they say, are fine soldiers too,
hurling javelins, shooting flights of arrows,
charioteers who can turn the tide – like that! –
when the great leveler, War, brings on some deadlock.

So I cannot tell if the gods will sail me home again
or I'll go down out there, on the fields of Troy,
but all things here must rest in your control.
Watch over my father and mother in the palace,
just as now, or perhaps a little more,
when I am far from home.
But once you see the beard on the boy's cheek,
you wed the man you like, and leave your house behind.'
So my husband advised me then. Now it all comes true . . .
a night will come when a hateful marriage falls my lot –
this cursed life of mine! Zeus has torn away my joy.
But there's something else that mortifies me now.
Your way is a far cry from the time-honored way
of suitors locked in rivalry, striving to win
some noble woman, a wealthy man's daughter.
They bring in their own calves and lambs
to feast the friends of the bride-to-be, yes,
and shower her with gleaming gifts as well.
They don't devour the woman's goods scot-free.'

    Staunch Odysseus glowed with joy to hear all this –
his wife's trickery luring gifts from her suitors now,
enchanting their hearts with suave seductive words

                                        'Gifts?'

but all the while with something else in mind.
Eupithes' son Antinous took her point at once.
'Daughter of Icarius, sensible Penelope,
whatever gifts your suitors would like to bring,
accept them. How ungracious to turn those gifts away!
We won't go back to our own estates, or anywhere else,
till you have wed the man you find the best.'

So he proposed, and all the rest agreed.
Each suitor sent a page to go and get a gift.
Antinous' man brought in a grand, resplendent robe,
stiff with embroidery, clasped with twelve gold brooches,
long pins that clipped into sheathing loops with ease.
Eurymachus' man brought in a necklace richly wrought,
gilded, strung with amber and glowing like the sun.
Eurydamas' two men came with a pair of earrings,
mulberry clusters dangling in triple drops
with a glint to catch the heart.
From the halls of lord Pisander, Polyctor's son,
a servant brought a choker, a fine, gleaming treasure.
And so each suitor in turn laid on a handsome gift.
Then the noble queen withdrew to her upper room,
her file of waiting ladies close behind her,
bearing the gorgeous presents in their arms.

Now the suitors turned to dance and song,
to the lovely beat and sway,
waiting for dusk to come upon them there . . .
and the dark night came upon them, lost in pleasure.
They rushed to set up three braziers along the walls
to give them light, piled them high with kindling,
sere, well-seasoned, just split with an ax,
and mixed in chips to keep the torches flaring.
The maids of Odysseus, steady man, took turns,
to keep the fires up, but the king himself,
dear to the gods and cunning to the core,
gave them orders brusquely: 'Maids of Odysseus,
your master gone so long – quick now, off you go
to the room where your queen and mistress waits.

Sit with her there and try to lift her spirits,
combing wool in your hands or spinning yarn.
But I will trim the torches for all her suitors,
even if they would like to revel on till Morning
mounts her throne. They'll never wear me down.
I have a name for lasting out the worst.'

                                                    At that
the women burst into laughter, glancing back and forth.
Flushed with beauty, Melantho mocked him shamelessly –
Dolius was her father but Penelope brought her up;
she treated her like her own child and gave her toys
to cheer her heart. But despite that, her heart
felt nothing for all her mistress' anguish now.
She was Eurymachus' lover, always slept with him.
She was the one who mocked her king and taunted,
'Cock of the walk, did someone beat your brains out?
Why not go bed down at the blacksmith's cozy forge?
Or a public place where tramps collect? Why here –
blithering on, nonstop,
bold as brass in the face of all these lords?
No fear in your heart? Wine's got to your wits? –
or do you always play the fool and babble nonsense?
Lost your head, have you, because you drubbed that hobo Irus?
You wait – a better man than Irus will take you on,
he'll box both sides of your skull with heavy fists
and cart you from the palace gushing blood!'

                                              '*You* wait,
you bitch' – the hardened veteran flashed a killing look.
'I'll go straight to the prince with your foul talk.
The prince will chop you to pieces here and now!'

His fury sent the women fluttering off, scattering
down the hall with panic shaking every limb –
they knew he spoke the truth.
But he took up his post by the flaring braziers,
tending the fires closely, looking after them all,
though the heart inside him stirred with other things,
ranging ahead, now, to all that must be done . . .

But Athena had no mind to let the brazen suitors
hold back now from their heart-rending insults –
she meant to make the anguish cut still deeper
into the core of Laertes' son Odysseus.
Polybus' son Eurymachus launched in first,
baiting the king to give his friends a laugh:
'Listen to me, you lords who court our noble queen!
I simply have to say what's on my mind. Look,
surely the gods have fetched this beggar here
to Odysseus' house. At least our torchlight *seems*
to come from the sheen of the man's own head –
there's not a hair on his bald pate, not a wisp!'

Then he wheeled on Odysseus, raider of cities:
'Stranger, how would you like to work for me
if I took you on – I'd give you decent wages –
picking the stones to lay a tight dry wall
or planting tall trees on the edge of my estate?
I'd give you rations to last you year-round,
clothes for your body, sandals for your feet.
Oh no, you've learned your lazy ways too well,
you've got no itch to stick to good hard work,

you'd rather go scrounging round the countryside,
begging for crusts to stuff your greedy gut!'

   'Ah, Eurymachus,' Odysseus, master of many exploits,
answered firmly, 'if only the two of us *could* go
man-to-man in the labors of the field . . .
In the late spring, when the long days come round,
out in the meadow, I swinging a well-curved scythe
and you swinging yours – we'd test our strength for work,
fasting right till dusk with lots of hay to mow.
Or give us a team of oxen to drive, purebreds,
hulking, ruddy beasts, both lusty with fodder,
paired for age and pulling-power that never flags –
with four acres to work, the loam churning under the plow –
you'd see what a straight unbroken furrow I could cut you
     then.
Or if Zeus would bring some battle on – out of the blue,
this very day – and give me a shield and two spears
and a bronze helmet to fit this soldier's temples,
then you'd see me fight where front ranks clash –
no more mocking this belly of mine, not then.
Enough. You're sick with pride, you brutal fool.
No doubt you count yourself a great, powerful man
because you sport with a puny crowd, ill-bred to boot.
If only Odysseus came back home and stood right here,
in a flash you'd find those doors – broad as they are –
too cramped for your race to safety through the porch!'

   That made Eurymachus' fury seethe and burst –
he gave the beggar a dark look and let fly, 'You,
you odious – I'll make you pay for your ugly rant!

Bold as brass in the face of all these lords?
No fear in your heart? Wine's got to your wits? –
or do you always play the fool and babble nonsense?
Lost your head, have you, because you drubbed that hobo
    Irus?'

   As he shouted out he seized a stool, but Odysseus,
fearing the blow, crouched at Amphinomus' knees
as Eurymachus hurled and hit the wine-steward,
clipping his right hand –
his cup dropped, clattered along the floor
and flat on his back he went, groaning in the dust.
The suitors broke into uproar through the shadowed halls,
glancing at one another, trading angry outcries:
'Would to god this drifter had dropped dead –'

   'Anywhere else before he landed here!'

   'Then he'd never have loosed such pandemonium.'

   'Now we're squabbling over *beggars*!'
                               'No more joy
in the sumptuous feast . . .'
                             'Now riot rules the day!'

   But now Prince Telemachus dressed them down:
'Fools, you're out of your minds! No hiding it,
food and wine have gone to your heads. Some god
has got your blood up. Come, now you've eaten well
go home to bed – when the spirit moves, that is.
I, for one, I'll drive no guest away.'

So he declared. And they all bit their lips,
amazed the prince could speak with so much daring.
At last Amphinomus rose to take the floor,
the noted son of Nisus, King Aretias' grandson.
'Fair enough, my friends; when a man speaks well
we have no grounds for wrangling, no cause for abuse.
Hands off the stranger! And any other servant
in King Odysseus' palace. Come, steward,
pour first drops for the god in every cup;
let's make libations, then go home to bed.
The stranger? Leave him here in Odysseus' halls
and have his host, Telemachus, tend him well –
it's the prince's royal house the man has reached.'

So he said. His proposal pleased them all.
And gallant Mulius, a herald of Dulichion,
a friend-in-arms of lord Amphinomus too,
mixed the men a bowl and, hovering closely,
poured full rounds for all. They tipped cups
to the blissful gods and then, libations made,
they drank the heady wine to their hearts' content
and went their ways to bed, each suitor to his house.

2

Penelope and Her Guest

That left the great Odysseus waiting in his hall
as Athena helped him plot the slaughter of the suitors.
He turned at once to Telemachus, brisk with orders:
'Now we must stow the weapons out of reach, my boy,
all the arms and armor – and when the suitors miss them
and ask you questions, put them off with a winning story:
"I stowed them away, clear of the smoke. A far cry
from the arms Odysseus left when he went to Troy,
fire-damaged equipment, black with reeking fumes.
And a god reminded me of something darker too.
When you're in your cups a quarrel might break out,
you'd wound each other, shame your feasting here
and cast a pall on your courting.
Iron has powers to draw a man to ruin."'
    Telemachus did his father's will at once,
calling out to his old nurse Eurycleia: 'Quick,
dear one, close the women up in their own quarters,
till I can stow my father's weapons in the storeroom.
Splendid gear, lying about, neglected, black with soot
since Father sailed away. I was only a boy then.
Now I must safeguard them from the smoke.'

'High time, child,' the loving nurse replied.
'If only you'd bother to tend your whole house
and safeguard *all* your treasures. Tell me,

who's to fetch and carry the torch for you?
You won't let out the maids who'd light your way.'

    'Our friend here will,' Telemachus answered coolly.
'I won't put up with a man who shirks his work,
not if he takes his ration from my stores,
even if he's miles away from home.'

    That silenced the old nurse.
She barred the doors that led from the long hall –
and up they sprang, Odysseus and his princely son,
and began to carry off the helmets, studded shields
and pointed spears, and Pallas Athena strode before them,
lifting a golden lamp that cast a dazzling radiance round
        about.
'Father,' Telemachus suddenly burst out to Odysseus,
'oh what a marvel fills my eyes! Look, look there –
all the sides of the hall, the handsome crossbeams,
pinewood rafters, the tall columns towering –
all glow in my eyes like flaming fire!
Surely a god is here –
one of those who rule the vaulting skies!'

    'Quiet,' his father, the old soldier, warned him.
'Get a grip on yourself. No more questions now.
It's just the way of the gods who rule Olympus.
Off you go to bed. I'll stay here behind
to test the women, test your mother too.
She in her grief will ask me everything I know.'

Under the flaring torchlight, through the hall
Telemachus made his way to his own bedroom now,
where he always went when welcome sleep came on him.
There he lay tonight as well, till Dawn's first light.
That left the great king still waiting in his hall
as Athena helped him plot the slaughter of the suitors . . .

Now down from her chamber came reserved Penelope,
looking for all the world like Artemis or golden Aphrodite.
Close to the fire her women drew her favorite chair
with its whorls of silver and ivory, inlaid rings.
The craftsman who made it years ago, Icmalius,
added a footrest under the seat itself,
mortised into the frame,
and over it all was draped a heavy fleece.
Here Penelope took her place, discreet, observant.
The women, arms bared, pressing in from their quarters,
cleared away the tables, the heaped remains of the feast
and the cups from which the raucous lords had drunk.
Raking embers from the braziers onto the ground,
they piled them high again with seasoned wood,
providing light and warmth.
                                    And yet again
Melantho lashed out at Odysseus: 'You still here? –
you pest, slinking around the house all night,
leering up at the women?
Get out, you tramp – be glad of the food you got –
or we'll sling a torch at you, rout you out at once!'

A killing glance, and the old trooper countered,
'What's possessed you, woman? Why lay into me? Such abuse!

Just because I'm filthy, because I wear such rags,
roving round the country, living hand-to-mouth.
But it's fate that drives me on:
that's the lot of beggars, homeless drifters.
I too once lived in a lofty house that men admired;
rolling in wealth, I'd often give to a vagabond like myself,
whoever he was, whatever need had brought him to my door.
And crowds of servants I had, and lots of all it takes
to live the life of ease, to make men call you rich.
But Zeus ruined it all – god's will, no doubt.
So beware, woman, or one day you may lose it all,
all your glitter that puts your work-mates in the shade.
Or your mistress may just fly in a rage and dress you down
or Odysseus may return – there's still room for hope!
Or if he's dead as you think and never coming home,
well there's his son, Telemachus . . .
like father, like son – thanks to god Apollo.
No women's wildness here in the house escapes
the prince's eye. He's come of age at last.'

    So he warned, and alert Penelope heard him,
wheeled on the maid and tongue-lashed her smartly:
'Make no mistake, you brazen, shameless bitch,
none of your ugly work escapes me either –
you will pay for it with your life, you will!
How well you knew – you heard from my own lips –
that I meant to probe this stranger in our house
and ask about my husband . . . my heart breaks for him.'

    She turned to her housekeeper Eurynome and said,
'Now bring us a chair and spread it soft with fleece,

so our guest can sit and tell me his whole story
and hear me out as well.
I'd like to ask him questions, point by point.'

Eurynome bustled off to fetch a polished chair
and set it down and spread it soft with fleece.
Here Odysseus sat, the man of many trials,
as cautious Penelope began the conversation:
'Stranger, let me start our questioning myself . . .
Who are you? where are you from? your city? your
      parents?'

'My good woman,' Odysseus, master of craft, replied,
'no man on the face of the earth could find fault with *you*.
Your fame, believe me, has reached the vaulting skies.
Fame like a flawless king's who dreads the gods,
who governs a kingdom vast, proud and strong –
who upholds justice, true, and the black earth
bears wheat and barley, trees bow down with fruit
and the sheep drop lambs and never fail and the sea
teems with fish – thanks to his decent, upright rule,
and under his sovereign sway the people flourish.
So then, here in your house, ask me anything else
but don't, please, search out my birth, my land,
or you'll fill my heart to overflowing even more
as I bring back the past . . .
I am a man who's had his share of sorrows.
It's wrong for me, in someone else's house,
to sit here moaning and groaning, sobbing so –
it makes things worse, this grieving on and on.
One of your maids, or you yourself, might scold me,

think it's just the wine that had doused my wits
and made me drown in tears.'

  'No, no, stranger,' wise Penelope demurred,
'whatever form and feature I had, what praise I'd won,
the deathless gods destroyed that day the Achaeans
sailed away to Troy, my husband in their ships,
Odysseus – if *he* could return to tend my life
the renown I had would only grow in glory.
Now my life is torment . . .
look at the griefs some god has loosed against me!
All the nobles who rule the islands round about,
Dulichion, Same, and wooded Zacynthus too,
and all who lord it in sunny Ithaca itself –
they court me against my will, they lay waste my house.
So I pay no heed to strangers, suppliants at my door,
not even heralds out on their public errands here –
I yearn for Odysseus, always, my heart pines away.
They rush the marriage on, and I spin out my wiles.
A god from the blue it was inspired me first
to set up a great loom in our royal halls
and I began to weave, and the weaving finespun,
the yarns endless, and I would lead them on: "Young men,
my suitors, now that King Odysseus is no more,
go slowly, keen as you are to marry me, until
I can finish off this web . . .
so my weaving won't all fray and come to nothing.
This is a shroud for old lord Laertes, for that day
when the deadly fate that lays us out at last will take him
    down.
I dread the shame my countrywomen would heap upon me,

yes, if a man of such wealth should lie in state
without a shroud for cover.''
                                My very words,
and despite their pride and passion they believed me.
So by day I'd weave at my great and growing web –
by night, by the light of torches set beside me,
I would unravel all I'd done. Three whole years
I deceived them blind, seduced them with this scheme.
Then, when the wheeling seasons brought the fourth year on
and the months waned and the long days came round once
    more,
then, thanks to my maids – the shameless, reckless creatures –
the suitors caught me in the act, denounced me harshly.
So I finished it off. Against my will. They forced me.
And now I cannot escape a marriage, nor can I contrive
a deft way out. My parents urge me to tie the knot
and my son is galled as they squander his estate –
he sees it all. He's a grown man by now, equipped
to tend to his own royal house and tend it well:
Zeus grants my son that honor . . .
But for all that – now tell me who you are.
Where do you come from? You've hardly sprung
from a rock or oak like some old man of legend.'

    The master improviser answered, slowly,
'My lady . . . wife of Laertes' son, Odysseus,
will your questions about my family never end?
All right then. Here's my story. Even though
it plunges me into deeper grief than I feel now.
But that's the way of the world, when one has been
so far from home, so long away as I, roving over

many cities of men, enduring many hardships.
Still,

my story will tell you all you need to know.

There is a land called Crete . . .
ringed by the wine-dark sea with rolling whitecaps –
handsome country, fertile, thronged with people
well past counting – boasting ninety cities,
language mixing with language side-by-side.
First come the Achaeans, then the native Cretans,
hardy, gallant in action, then Cydonian clansmen,
Dorians living in three tribes, and proud Pelasgians last.
Central to all their cities is magnificent Cnossos,
the site where Minos ruled and each ninth year
conferred with almighty Zeus himself. Minos,
father of my father, Deucalion, that bold heart.
Besides myself Deucalion sired Prince Idomeneus,
who set sail for Troy in his beaked ships of war,
escorting Atreus' sons. My own name is Aethon.
I am the younger-born;
my older brother's a better man than I am.
Now, it was there in Cnossos that I saw him . . .
Odysseus – and we traded gifts of friendship.
A heavy gale had landed him on our coast,
driven him way off course, rounding Malea's cape
when he was bound for Troy. He anchored in Amnisus,
hard by the goddess' cave of childbirth and labor,
that rough harbor – barely riding out the storm.
He came into town at once, asking for Idomeneus,
claiming to be my brother's close, respected friend.
Too late. Ten or eleven days had already passed

since he set sail for Troy in his beaked ships.
So I took Odysseus back to my own house,
gave him a hero's welcome, treated him in style –
stores in our palace made for princely entertainment.
As for his comrades, all who'd shipped with him,
I dipped into public stock to give them barley,
ruddy wine and fine cattle for slaughter,
beef to their hearts' content. A dozen days
they stayed with me there, those brave Achaeans,
penned up by a North Wind so stiff that a man,
even on dry land, could never keep his feet –
some angry spirit raised that blast, I'd say.
Then on the thirteenth day the wind died down
and they set sail for Troy.'

                  Falsehoods all,
but he gave his falsehoods all the ring of truth.
As she listened on, her tears flowed and soaked her cheeks
as the heavy snow melts down from the high mountain
    ridges,
snow the West Wind piles there and the warm East Wind
    thaws
and the snow, melting, swells the rivers to overflow their
    banks –
so she dissolved in tears, streaming down her lovely cheeks,
weeping for him, her husband, sitting there beside her.
Odysseus' heart went out to his grief-stricken wife
but under his lids his eyes remained stock-still –
they might have been horn or iron –
his guile fought back his tears. And she,
once she'd had her fill of grief and weeping,
turned again to her guest with this reply:

'Now, stranger, I think I'll test you, just to see
if there in your house, with all his friends-in-arms,
you actually entertained my husband as you say.
Come, tell me what sort of clothing he wore,
what cut of man was he?
What of the men who followed in his train?'

                                        'Ah good woman,'
Odysseus, the great master of subtlety, returned,
'how hard it is to speak, after so much time
apart . . . why, some twenty years have passed
since he left my house and put my land behind him.
Even so, imagine the man as I portray him –
I can see him now.

                    King Odysseus . . .
he was wearing a heavy woolen cape, sea-purple
in double folds, with a golden brooch to clasp it,
twin sheaths for the pins, on the face a work of art:
a hound clenching a dappled fawn in its front paws,
slashing it as it writhed. All marveled to see it,
solid gold as it was, the hound slashing, throttling
the fawn in its death-throes, hoofs flailing to break free.
I noticed his glossy tunic too, clinging to his skin
like the thin glistening skin of a dried onion,
silky, soft, the glint of the sun itself.
Women galore would gaze on it with relish.
And this too. Bear it in mind, won't you?
I've no idea if Odysseus wore these things at home
or a comrade gave him them as he boarded ship,
or a host perhaps – the man was loved by many.
There were few Achaeans to equal him . . . and I?
I gave him a bronze sword myself, a lined cloak,

28

elegant, deep red, and a fringed shirt as well,
and I saw him off in his long benched ship of war
in lordly style.
                    Something else. He kept a herald
beside him, a man a little older than himself.
I'll try to describe him to you, best I can.
Round-shouldered he was, swarthy, curly-haired.
His name? Eurybates. And Odysseus prized him
most of all his men. Their minds worked as one.'

His words renewed her deep desire to weep,
recognizing the strong clear signs Odysseus offered.
But as soon as she'd had her fill of tears and grief,
Penelope turned again to her guest and said,
'Now, stranger, much as I pitied you before,
now in my house you'll be my special friend,
my honored guest. I am the one, myself,
who gave him the very clothes that you describe.
I brought them up from the storeroom, folded them neatly,
fastened the golden brooch to adorn my husband,
Odysseus – never again will I embrace him,
striding home to his own native land.
A black day it was
when he took ship to see that cursed city . . .
Destroy, I call it – I hate to say its name!'

'Ah my queen,' the man of craft assured her,
'noble wife of Laertes' son, Odysseus,
ravage no more your lovely face with tears
or consume your heart with grieving for your husband.
Not that I'd blame you, ever. Any woman will mourn

the bridegroom she has lost, lain with in love
and borne his children too. Even though he
was no Odysseus – a man like a god, they say.
But dry your tears and take my words to heart.
I will tell you the whole truth and hide nothing:
I have heard that Odysseus now, at last, is on his way,
he's just in reach, in rich Thesprotian country –
the man is still alive
and he's bringing home a royal hoard of treasure,
gifts he won from the people of those parts.
His crew? He's lost his crew and hollow ship
on the wine-dark waters off Thrinacia Island.
Zeus and Helios raged, dead set against Odysseus
for his men-at-arms had killed the cattle of the Sun,
so down to the last hand they drowned in crashing seas.
But not Odysseus, clinging tight to his ship's keel –
the breakers flung him out onto dry land, on Scheria,
the land of Phaeacians, close kin to the gods themselves,
and with all their hearts they prized him like a god,
showered the man with gifts, and they'd have gladly
sailed him home unscathed. In fact Odysseus
would have been here beside you long ago
but he thought it the better, shrewder course
to recoup his fortunes roving through the world.
At sly profit-turning there's not a man alive
to touch Odysseus. He's got no rival there.
So I learned from Phidon, king of Thesprotia,
who swore to me as he poured libations in his house,
"The ship's hauled down and the shipmates set to sail,
to take Odysseus home to native land."

But I . . .

he shipped me off before. A Thesprotian cutter
chanced to be heading for Dulichion rich in wheat.
But he showed me all the treasure Odysseus had amassed,
enough to last a man and ten generations of his heirs –
so great the wealth stored up for *him* in the king's vaults!
But Odysseus, he made clear, was off at Dodona then
to hear the will of Zeus that rustles forth
from the god's tall leafy oak: how should he return,
after all the years away, to his own beloved Ithaca,
openly or in secret?

                And so the man is safe,
as you can see, and he's coming home, soon,
he's close, close at hand –
he won't be severed long from kin and country,
no, not now. I give you my solemn, binding oath.
I swear by Zeus, the first, the greatest god –
by Odysseus' hearth, where I have come for help:
all will come to pass, I swear, exactly as I say.
True, this very month – just as the old moon dies
and the new moon rises into life – Odysseus will return!'

  'If only, my friend,' reserved Penelope exclaimed,
'everything you say would come to pass!
You'd soon know my affection, know my gifts.
Any man you meet would call you blest.
But my heart can sense the way it all will go.
Odysseus, I tell you, is never coming back,
nor will you ever gain your passage home,
for we have no masters in our house like him
at welcoming in or sending off an honored guest.
Odysseus. There was a man, or was he all a dream?

31

But come, women, wash the stranger and make his bed,
with bedding, blankets and lustrous spreads to keep him
      warm
till Dawn comes up and takes her golden throne.
Then, tomorrow at daybreak, bathe him well
and rub him down with oil, so he can sit beside
Telemachus in the hall, enjoy his breakfast there.
And anyone who offends our guest beyond endurance –
he defeats himself; he's doomed to failure here,
no matter how raucously he raves and blusters on.
For how can you know, my friend, if I surpass
all women in thoughtfulness and shrewd good sense,
if I'd allow you to take your meals at hall
so weatherbeaten, clad in rags and tatters?
Our lives are much too brief . . .
If a man is cruel by nature, cruel in action,
the mortal world will call down curses on his head
while he is alive, and all will mock his memory after death.
But then if a man is kind by nature, kind in action,
his guests will carry his fame across the earth
and people all will praise him from the heart.'

   'Wait, my queen,' the crafty man objected,
'noble wife of Laertes' son, Odysseus –
blankets and glossy spreads? They're not my style.
Not from the day I launched out in my long-oared ship
and the snowy peaks of Crete went fading far astern.
I'll lie as I've done through sleepless nights before.
Many a night I've spent on rugged beds afield,
waiting for Dawn to mount her lovely throne.
Nor do I pine for any footbaths either.

Of all the women who serve your household here,
not one will touch my feet. Unless, perhaps,
there is some old retainer, the soul of trust,
someone who's borne as much as I have borne . . .
I wouldn't mind if she would touch my feet.'

                         'Dear friend,'
the discreet Penelope replied, 'never has any man
so thoughtful – of all the guests in my palace
come from foreign parts – been as welcome as you . . .
so sensible, so apt, is every word you say.
I have just such an old woman, seasoned, wise,
who carefully tended my unlucky husband, reared him,
took him into her arms the day his mother bore him –
frail as the woman is, she'll wash your feet.
Up with you now, my good old Eurycleia,
come and wash your master's . . . equal in years.
Odysseus must have feet and hands like his by now –
hardship can age a person overnight.'

                             At that name
the old retainer buried her face in both hands,
burst into warm tears and wailed out in grief,
'Oh my child, how helpless I am to help you now!
How Zeus despised you, more than all other men,
god-fearing man that you were . . .
Never did any mortal burn the Old Thunderer
such rich thighbones – offerings charred and choice –
never as many as *you* did, praying always to reach
a ripe old age and raise a son to glory. Now,
you alone he's robbed of your home-coming day!
Just so, the women must have mocked my king,
far away, when he'd stopped at some fine house –

just as all these bitches, stranger, mock you here.
And because you shrink from their taunts, their wicked
    barbs,
you will not let them wash you. The work is mine –
Icarius' daughter, wise Penelope, bids me now
and I am all too glad. I will wash your feet,
both for my own dear queen and for yourself –
your sorrows wring my heart . . . and why?
Listen to me closely, mark my words.
Many a wayworn guest has landed here
but never, I swear, has one so struck my eyes –
your build, your voice, your feet – you're like Odysseus . . .
to the life!'

       'Old woman,' wily Odysseus countered,
'that's what they all say who've seen us both.
We bear a striking resemblance to each other,
as you have had the wit to say yourself.'

   The old woman took up a burnished basin
she used for washing feet and poured in bowls
of fresh cold water before she stirred in hot.
Odysseus, sitting full in the firelight, suddenly
swerved round to the dark, gripped by a quick misgiving –
soon as she touched him she might spot the scar!
The truth would all come out.

              Bending closer
she started to bathe her master . . . then,
in a flash, she knew the scar –

              that old wound
made years ago by a boar's white tusk when Odysseus
went to Parnassus, out to see Autolycus and his sons.

The man was his mother's noble father, one who excelled
the world at thievery, that and subtle, shifty oaths.
Hermes gave him the gift, overjoyed by the thighs
of lambs and kids he burned in the god's honor –
Hermes the ready partner in his crimes. Now,
Autolycus once visited Ithaca's fertile land,
to find his daughter's son had just been born.
Eurycleia set him down on the old man's knees
as he finished dinner, urging him, 'Autolycus,
you must find a name for your daughter's darling son.
The baby comes as the answer to her prayers.'

                                      'You,
my daughter, and you, my son-in-law,' Autolycus replied,
'give the boy the name I tell you now. Just as I
have come from afar, creating pain for many –
men and women across the good green earth –
so let his name be *Odysseus* . . .
the Son of Pain, a name he'll earn in full.
And when he has come of age and pays his visit
to Parnassus – the great estate of his mother's line
where all my treasures lie – I will give him enough
to cheer his heart, then speed him home to you.'

                                            And so,
in time, Odysseus went to collect the splendid gifts.
Autolycus and the sons of Autolycus warmed him in
with eager handclasps, hearty words of welcome.
His mother's mother, Amphithea, hugged the boy
and kissed his face and kissed his shining eyes.
Autolycus told his well-bred sons to prepare
a princely feast. They followed orders gladly,
herded an ox inside at once, five years old,

skinned it and split the carcass into quarters,
deftly cut it in pieces, skewered these on spits,
roasted all to a turn and served the portions out.
So all day long till the sun went down they feasted,
consuming equal shares to their hearts' content.
Then when the sun had set and night came on
they turned to bed and took the gift of sleep.

                                    As soon
as young Dawn with her rose-red fingers shone once more
they all moved out for the hunt, hounds in the lead,
Autolycus' sons and Prince Odysseus in their ranks.
Climbing Parnassus' ridges, thick with timber,
they quickly reached the mountain's windy folds
and just as the sun began to strike the plowlands,
rising out of the deep calm flow of the Ocean River,
the beaters came to a wooded glen, the hounds broke,
hot on a trail, and right behind the pack they came,
Autolycus' sons – Odysseus out in front now,
pressing the dogs, brandishing high his spear
with its long shadow waving. Then and there
a great boar lay in wait, in a thicket lair so dense
that the sodden gusty winds could never pierce it,
nor could the sun's sharp rays invade its depths
nor a downpour drench it through and through,
so dense, so dark, and piled with fallen leaves.
Here, as the hunters closed in for the kill,
crowding the hounds, the tramp of men and dogs
came drumming round the boar – he crashed from his lair,
his razor back bristling, his eyes flashing fire
and charging up to the hunt he stopped, at bay –
and Odysseus rushed him first,

shaking his long spear in a sturdy hand,
wild to strike but the boar struck faster,
lunging in on the slant, a tusk thrusting up
over the boy's knee, gouging a deep strip of flesh
but it never hit the bone –

                        Odysseus thrust and struck,
stabbing the beast's right shoulder –

                                a glint of bronze –
the point ripped clean through and down in the dust he
   dropped,
grunting out his breath as his life winged away.
The sons of Autolycus, working over Odysseus,
skillfully binding up his open wound –
the gallant, godlike prince –
chanted an old spell that stanched the blood
and quickly bore him home to their father's palace.
There, in no time, Autolycus and the sons of Autolycus
healed him well and, showering him with splendid gifts,
sped Odysseus back to his native land, to Ithaca,
a young man filled with joy. His happy parents,
his father and noble mother, welcomed him home
and asked him of all his exploits, blow-by-blow:
how did he get that wound? He told his tale with style,
how the white tusk of a wild boar had gashed his leg,
hunting on Parnassus with Autolycus and his sons . . .

                                    That scar –
as the old nurse cradled his leg and her hands passed down
she felt it, knew it, suddenly let his foot fall –
down it dropped in the basin – the bronze clanged,
tipping over, spilling water across the floor.
Joy and torment gripped her heart at once,

tears rushed to her eyes – voice choked in her throat
she reached for Odysseus' chin and whispered quickly,
'Yes, yes! you are *Odysseus* – oh dear boy –
I couldn't know you before . . .
not till I touched the body of my king!'

   She glanced at Penelope, keen to signal her
that here was her own dear husband, here and now,
but she could not catch the glance, she took no heed,
Athena turned her attention elsewhere. But Odysseus –
his right hand shot out, clutching the nurse's throat,
with his left he hugged her to himself and muttered,
'Nurse, you want to kill me? You suckled me yourself
at your own breast – and now I'm home, at last,
after bearing twenty years of brutal hardship,
home, on native ground. But now you know,
now that a god has flashed it in your mind,
quiet! not a word to anyone in the house.
Or else, I warn you – and I mean business too –
if a god beats down these brazen suitors at my hands,
I will not spare you – my old nurse that you are –
when I kill the other women in my house.'

   'Child,' shrewd old Eurycleia protested,
'what nonsense you let slip through your teeth!
You know *me* – I'm stubborn, never give an inch –
I'll keep still as solid rock or iron.
One more thing. Take it to heart, I tell you.
If a god beats down these brazen suitors at your hands,
I'll report in full on the women in your house:
who are disloyal to you, who are guiltless.'

'Nurse,' the cool tactician Odysseus said,
'why bother to count them off? A waste of breath.
I'll observe them, judge each one myself.
Just be quiet. Keep your tales to yourself.
Leave the rest to the gods.'
                                        Hushed so,
the old nurse went padding along the halls
to fetch more water – her basin had all spilled –
and once she'd bathed and rubbed him down with oil,
Odysseus drew his chair up near the fire again,
trying to keep warm,
but he hid his scar beneath his beggar's rags
as cautious Penelope resumed their conversation:
'My friend, I have only one more question for you,
something slight, now the hour draws on for welcome
        sleep –
for those who can yield to sweet repose, that is,
heartsick as they are. As for myself, though,
some god has sent me pain that knows no bounds.
All day long I indulge myself in sighs and tears
as I see to my tasks, direct the household women.
When night falls and the world lies lost in sleep,
I take to my bed, my heart throbbing, about to break,
anxieties swarming, piercing – I may go mad with grief.
Like Pandareus' daughter, the nightingale in the green
        woods
lifting her lovely song at the first warm rush of spring,
perched in the treetops' rustling leaves and pouring forth
her music shifting, trilling and sinking, rippling high to burst
in grief for Itylus, her beloved boy, King Zethus' son
whom she in innocence once cut down with bronze . . .

so my wavering heart goes shuttling, back and forth:
Do I stay beside my son and keep all things secure –
my lands, my serving-women, the grand high-roofed house –
true to my husband's bed, the people's voice as well?
Or do I follow, at last, the best man who courts me
here in the halls, who gives the greatest gifts?
My son – when he was a boy and lighthearted –
urged me not to marry and leave my husband's house.
But now he has grown and reached his young prime,
he begs me to leave our palace, travel home.
Telemachus, so obsessed with his own estate,
the wealth my princely suitors bleed away.

                                        But please,
read this dream for me, won't you? Listen closely . . .
I keep twenty geese in the house, from the water trough
they come and peck their wheat – I love to watch them all.
But down from a mountain swooped this great hook-beaked
    eagle,
yes, and he snapped their necks and killed them one and all
and they lay in heaps throughout the halls while he,
back to the clear blue sky he soared at once.
But I wept and wailed – only a dream, of course –
and our well-groomed ladies came and clustered round me,
sobbing, stricken: the eagle killed my geese. But down
he swooped again and settling onto a jutting rafter
called out in a human voice that dried my tears,
"Courage, daughter of famous King Icarius!
This is no dream but a happy waking vision,
real as day, that will come true for you.
The geese were your suitors – I was once the eagle
but now I am your husband, back again at last,

40

about to launch a terrible fate against them all!''
So he vowed, and the soothing sleep released me.
I peered around and saw my geese in the house,
pecking at their wheat, at the same trough
where they always took their meal.'

                      'Dear woman,'
quick Odysseus answered, 'twist it however you like,
your dream can only mean one thing. Odysseus
told you himself – he'll make it come to pass.
Destruction is clear for each and every suitor;
not a soul escapes his death and doom.'

  'Ah my friend,' seasoned Penelope dissented,
'dreams are hard to unravel, wayward, drifting things –
not all we glimpse in them will come to pass . . .
Two gates there are for our evanescent dreams,
one is made of ivory, the other made of horn.
Those that pass through the ivory cleanly carved
are will-o'-the-wisps, their message bears no fruit.
The dreams that pass through the gates of polished horn
are fraught with truth, for the dreamer who can see them.
But I can't believe my strange dream has come that way,
much as my son and I would love to have it so.
One more thing I'll tell you – weigh it well.
The day that dawns today, this cursed day,
will cut me off from Odysseus' house. Now,
I mean to announce a contest with those axes,
the ones he would often line up here inside the hall,
twelve in a straight unbroken row like blocks to shore a keel,
then stand well back and whip an arrow through the lot.
Now I will bring them on as a trial for my suitors.

The hand that can string the bow with greatest ease,
that shoots an arrow clean through all twelve axes –
he's the man I follow, yes, forsaking this house
where I was once a bride, this gracious house
so filled with the best that life can offer –
I shall always remember it, that I know . . .
even in my dreams.'

                'Oh my queen,'
Odysseus, man of exploits, urged her on,
'royal wife of Laertes' son, Odysseus, now,
don't put off this test in the halls a moment.
Before that crew can handle the polished bow,
string it taut and shoot through all those axes –
Odysseus, man of exploits, will be home with you!'

   'If only, my friend,' the wise Penelope replied,
'you were willing to sit beside me in the house,
indulging me in the comfort of your presence,
sleep would never drift across my eyes.
But one can't go without one's sleep forever.
The immortals give each thing its proper place
in our mortal lives throughout the good green earth.
So now I'm going back to my room upstairs
and lie down on my bed,
that bed of pain my tears have streaked, year in,
year out, from the day Odysseus sailed away to see . . .
Destroy, I call it – I hate to say its name!
There I'll rest, while you lie here in the hall,
spreading your blankets somewhere on the floor,
or the women will prepare a decent bed.'

                    With that

the queen went up to her lofty well-lit room
and not alone: her women followed close behind.
Penelope, once they reached the upper story,
fell to weeping for Odysseus, her beloved husband,
till watchful Athena sealed her eyes with welcome sleep.

3

Portents Gather

Off in the entrance-hall the great king made his bed,
spreading out on the ground the raw hide of an ox,
heaping over it fleece from sheep the suitors
butchered day and night, then Eurynome threw
a blanket over him, once he'd nestled down.
And there Odysseus lay . . .
plotting within himself the suitors' death –
awake, alert, as the women slipped from the house,
the maids who whored in the suitors' beds each night,
tittering, linking arms and frisking as before.
The master's anger rose inside his chest,
torn in thought, debating, head and heart –
should he up and rush them, kill them one and all
or let them rut with their lovers one last time?
The heart inside him growled low with rage,
as a bitch mounting over her weak, defenseless puppies
growls, facing a stranger, bristling for a showdown –
so he growled from his depths, hackles rising at their outrage.
But he struck his chest and curbed his fighting heart:
'Bear up, old heart! You've borne worse, far worse,
that day when the Cyclops, man-mountain, bolted
your hardy comrades down. But you held fast –
Nobody but your cunning pulled you through
the monster's cave you thought would be your death.'

So he forced his spirit into submission,
the rage in his breast reined back – unswerving,
all endurance. But he himself kept tossing, turning,
intent as a cook before some white-hot blazing fire
who rolls his sizzling sausage back and forth,
packed with fat and blood – keen to broil it quickly,
tossing, turning it, this way, that way – so he cast about;
how could he get these shameless suitors in his clutches,
one man facing a mob? . . . when close to his side she came,
Athena sweeping down from the sky in a woman's build
and hovering at his head, the goddess spoke:
'Why still awake? The unluckiest man alive!
Here is your house, your wife at home, your son,
as fine a boy as one could hope to have.'

                                                    'True,'
the wily fighter replied, 'how right you are, goddess,
but still this worry haunts me, heart and soul –
how can I get these shameless suitors in my clutches?
Single-handed, braving an army always camped inside.
There's another worry, that haunts me even more.
What if I kill them – thanks to you and Zeus –
how do I run from under their avengers?
Show me the way, I ask you.'

                                                    'Impossible man!'
Athena bantered, the goddess' eyes ablaze.
'Others are quick to trust a weaker comrade,
some poor mortal, far less cunning than I.
But I am a goddess, look, the very one who
guards you in all your trials to the last.
I tell you this straight out:
even if fifty bands of mortal fighters

closed around us, hot to kill us off in battle,
still you could drive away their herds and sleek flocks!
So, surrender to sleep at last. What a misery,
keeping watch through the night, wide awake –
you'll soon come up from under all your troubles.'

    With that she showered sleep across his eyes
and back to Olympus went the lustrous goddess.
As soon as sleep came on him, loosing his limbs,
slipping the toils of anguish from his mind,
his devoted wife awoke and,
sitting up in her soft bed, returned to tears.
When the queen had wept to her heart's content
she prayed to the Huntress, Artemis, first of all:
'Artemis – goddess, noble daughter of Zeus, if only
you'd whip an arrow through my breast and tear my life out,
now, at once! Or let some whirlwind pluck me up
and sweep me away along those murky paths and
fling me down where the Ocean River running
round the world rolls back upon itself!
                                                Quick
as the whirlwinds swept away Pandareus' daughters –
years ago, when the gods destroyed their parents,
leaving the young girls orphans in their house.
But radiant Aphrodite nursed them well
on cheese and luscious honey and heady wine,
and Hera gave them beauty and sound good sense,
more than all other women – virgin Artemis made them tall
and Athena honed their skills to fashion lovely work.
But then, when Aphrodite approached Olympus' peaks
to ask for the girls their crowning day as brides

from Zeus who loves the lightning – Zeus who knows all,
all that's fated, all not fated, for mortal man –
then the storm spirits snatched them away
and passed them on to the hateful Furies,
yes, for all their loving care.

                 Just so
may the gods who rule Olympus blot me out!
Artemis with your glossy braids, come shoot me dead –
so I can plunge beneath this loathsome earth
with the image of Odysseus vivid in my mind.
Never let me warm the heart of a weaker man!
Even grief is bearable, true, when someone weeps
through the days, sobbing, heart convulsed with pain
yet embraced by sleep all night – sweet oblivion, sleep
dissolving all, the good and the bad, once it seals our eyes –
but even my dreams torment me, sent by wicked spirits.
Again – just this night – someone lay beside me . . .
like Odysseus to the life, when he embarked
with his men-at-arms. My heart raced with joy.
No dream, I thought, the waking truth at last!'

                          At those words
Dawn rose on her golden throne in a sudden gleam of light.
And great Odysseus caught the sound of his wife's cry
and began to daydream – deep in his heart it seemed
she stood beside him, knew him, now, at last . . .
Gathering up the fleece and blankets where he'd slept,
he laid them on a chair in the hall, he took the oxhide out
and spread it down, lifted his hands and prayed to Zeus:
'Father Zeus, if you really willed it so – to bring me
home over land and sea-lanes, home to native ground
after all the pain you brought me – show me a sign,

a good omen voiced by someone awake indoors,
another sign, outside, from Zeus himself!'

    And Zeus in all his wisdom heard that prayer.
He thundered at once, out of his clear blue heavens
high above the clouds, and Odysseus' spirit lifted.
Then from within the halls a woman grinding grain
let fly a lucky word. Close at hand she was,
where the good commander set the handmills once
and now twelve women in all performed their tasks,
grinding the wheat and barley, marrow of men's bones.
The rest were abed by now – they'd milled their stint –
this one alone, the frailest of all, kept working on.
Stopping her mill, she spoke an omen for her master:
'Zeus, Father! King of gods and men, now *there*
was a crack of thunder out of the starry sky –
and not a cloud in sight!
Sure it's a sign you're showing someone now.
So, poor as I am, grant *me* my prayer as well:
let this day be the last, the last these suitors
bolt their groaning feasts in King Odysseus' house!
These brutes who break my knees – heart-wrenching labor,
grinding their grain – now let them eat their last!'

    A lucky omen, linked with Zeus's thunder.
Odysseus' heart leapt up, the man convinced
he'd grind the scoundrels' lives out in revenge.
                             By now
the other maids were gathering in Odysseus' royal palace,
raking up on the hearth the fire still going strong.
Telemachus climbed from bed and dressed at once,

brisk as a young god –
over his shoulder he slung his well-honed sword,
he fastened rawhide sandals under his smooth feet,
he seized his tough spear tipped with a bronze point
and took his stand at the threshold, calling Eurycleia:
'Dear nurse, how did you treat the stranger in our house?
With bed and board? Or leave him to lie untended?
That would be mother's way – sensible as she is –
all impulse, doting over some worthless stranger,
turning a good man out to face the worst.'

   'Please, child,' his calm old nurse replied,
'don't blame *her* – your mother's blameless this time.
He sat and drank his wine till he'd had his fill.
Food? He'd lost his hunger. But she asked him.
And when it was time to think of turning in,
she told the maids to spread a decent bed, but he –
so down-and-out, poor soul, so dogged by fate –
said no to snuggling into a bed, between covers.
No sir, the man lay down in the entrance-hall,
on the raw hide of an ox and sheep's fleece,
and we threw a blanket over him, so we did.'

                      Hearing that,
Telemachus strode out through the palace, spear in hand,
and a pair of sleek hounds went trotting at his heels.
He made for the meeting grounds to join the island lords
while Eurycleia the daughter of Ops, Pisenor's son,
that best of women, gave the maids their orders:
'Quick now, look alive, sweep out the house,
wet down the floors!

            You, those purple coverlets,

fling them over the fancy chairs!
All those tables,
sponge them down – scour the winebowls, burnished cups!
The rest – now off you go to the spring and fetch some water,
fast as your legs can run!
Our young gallants won't be long from the palace,
they'll be bright and early – today's a public feast.'

   They hung on her words and ran to do her bidding.
Full twenty scurried off to the spring's dark water,
others bent to the housework, all good hands.
Then in they trooped, the strutting serving-men,
who split the firewood cleanly now as the women
bustled in from the spring, the swineherd at their heels,
driving three fat porkers, the best of all his herds.
And leaving them to root in the broad courtyard,
up he went to Odysseus, hailed him warmly:
'Friend, do the suitors show you more respect
or treat you like the dregs of the earth as always?'

   'Good Eumaeus,' the crafty man replied,
'if only the gods would pay back their outrage!
Wild and reckless young cubs, conniving here
in another's house. They've got no sense of shame.'

   And now as the two confided in each other,
the goatherd Melanthius sauntered toward them,
herding his goats with a pair of drovers' help,
the pick of his flocks to make the suitors' meal.
Under the echoing porch he tethered these, then turned
on Odysseus once again with cutting insults: 'Still alive?

Still hounding your betters, begging round the house?
Why don't you cart yourself away? Get out!
We'll never part, I swear,
till we taste each other's fists. Riffraff,
you and your begging make us sick! Get out –
we're hardly the only banquet on the island.'

No reply. The wily one just shook his head,
silent, his mind churning with thoughts of bloody work . . .

Third to arrive was Philoetius, that good cowherd,
prodding in for the crowd a heifer and fat goats.
Boatmen had brought them over from the mainland,
crews who ferry across all travelers too,
whoever comes for passage.
Under the echoing porch he tethered all heads well
and then approached the swineherd, full of questions:
'Who's this stranger, Eumaeus, just come to the house?
What roots does the man claim – who are his people?
Where are his blood kin? his father's fields?
Poor beggar. But what a build – a royal king's!
Ah, once the gods weave trouble into our lives
they drive us across the earth, they drown us all in pain,
even kings of the realm.'
                                        And with that thought
he walked up to Odysseus, gave him his right hand
and winged a greeting: 'Cheers, old friend, old father,
here's to your luck, great days from this day on –
saddled now as you are with so much trouble.
Father Zeus, no god's more deadly than you!
No mercy for men, you give them life yourself

then plunge them into misery, brutal hardship.
I broke into sweat, my friend, when I first saw you –
see, my eyes still brim with tears, remembering *him*,
Odysseus . . . He must wear such rags, I know it,
knocking about, drifting through the world
if he's still alive and sees the light of day.
If he's dead already, lost in the House of Death,
my heart aches for Odysseus, my great lord and master.
He set me in charge of his herds, in Cephallenian country,
when I was just a youngster. How they've grown by now,
past counting! No mortal on earth could breed
a finer stock of oxen – broad in the brow,
they thrive like ears of corn. But just look,
these interlopers tell me to drive them in
for their own private feasts. Not a thought
for the young prince in the house, they never flinch –
no regard for the gods' wrath – in their mad rush
to carve up his goods, my master gone so long!
I'm tossed from horn to horn in my own mind . . .
What a traitor I'd be, with the prince still alive,
if I'd run off to some other country, herds and all,
to a new set of strangers. Ah, but isn't it worse
to hold out here, tending the herds for upstarts,
not their owners – suffering all the pains of hell?
I could have fled, ages ago, to some great king
who'd give me shelter. It's unbearable here.
True, but I still dream of my old master,
unlucky man – if only *he*'d drop in from the blue
and drive these suitors all in a rout throughout the halls!'

'Cowherd,' the cool tactician Odysseus answered,
'you're no coward, and nobody's fool, I'd say.
Even I can see there's sense in that old head.
So I tell you this on my solemn, binding oath:
I swear by Zeus, the first of all the gods –
by the table of hospitality waiting for us,
by Odysseus' hearth where I have come for help,
Odysseus will come home while you're still here.
You'll see with your own eyes, if you have the heart,
these suitors who lord it here cut down in blood.'

'Stranger, if only,' the cowherd cried aloud,
'if only Zeus would make that oath come true –
you'd see my power, my fighting arms in action!'

Eumaeus echoed his prayer to all the gods
that their wise king would soon come home again.

Now as they spoke and urged each other on,
and once more the suitors were plotting certain doom
for the young prince – suddenly, banking high on the left
an omen flew past, an eagle clutching a trembling dove.
And Amphinomus rose in haste to warn them all,
'My friends, we'll never carry off this plot
to kill the prince. Let's concentrate on feasting.'

His timely invitation pleased them all.
The suitors ambled into Odysseus' royal house
and flinging down their cloaks on a chair or bench,
they butchered hulking sheep and fatted goats,
full-grown hogs and a young cow from the herd.

They roasted all the innards, served them round
and filled the bowls with wine and mixed it well.
Eumaeus passed out cups; Philoetius, trusty herdsman,
brought on loaves of bread in ample wicker trays;
Melanthius poured the wine. The whole company
reached out for the good things that lay at hand.

Telemachus, maneuvering shrewdly, sat his father down
on the stone threshold, just inside the timbered hall,
and set a rickety stool and cramped table there.
He gave him a share of innards, poured his wine
in a golden cup and added a bracing invitation:
'Now sit right there. Drink your wine with the crowd.
I'll defend you from all their taunts and blows,
these young bucks. This is no public place,
this is *Odysseus'* house –
my father won it for me, so it's mine.
You suitors, control yourselves. No insults now,
no brawling, no, or it's war between us all.'

So he declared. And they all bit their lips,
amazed the prince could speak with so much daring.
Only Eupithes' son Antinous ventured,
'Fighting words, but do let's knuckle under –
to our *prince*. Such abuse, such naked threats!
But clearly Zeus has foiled us. Or long before
we would have shut his mouth for him in the halls,
fluent and flowing as he is.'

                              So he mocked.
Telemachus paid no heed.

                              And now through the streets

the heralds passed, leading the beasts marked out
for sacrifice on Apollo's grand festal day,
and the islanders with their long hair were filing
into the god's shady grove – the distant deadly Archer.

    Those in the palace, once they'd roasted the prime cuts,
pulled them off the spits and, sharing out the portions,
fell to the royal feast . . .
The men who served them gave Odysseus his share,
as fair as the helping they received themselves.
So Telemachus ordered, the king's own son.

    But Athena had no mind to let the brazen suitors
hold back now from their heart-rending insults –
she meant to make the anguish cut still deeper
into the core of Laertes' son Odysseus.
There was one among them, a lawless boor –
Ctesippus was his name, he made his home in Same,
a fellow so impressed with his own astounding wealth
he courted the wife of Odysseus, gone for years.
Now the man harangued his swaggering comrades:
'Listen to me, my fine friends, here's what I say!
From the start our guest has had his fair share –
it's only right, you know.
How impolite it would be, how wrong to scant
whatever guest Telemachus welcomes to his house.
Look here, I'll give him a proper guest-gift too,
a prize he can hand the crone who bathes his feet
or a tip for another slave who haunts the halls
of our great King Odysseus!'
                        On that note,

grabbing an oxhoof out of a basket where it lay,
with a brawny hand he flung it straight at the king –
but Odysseus ducked his head a little, dodging the blow,
and seething just as the oxhoof hit the solid wall
he clenched his teeth in a wry sardonic grin.
Telemachus dressed Ctesippus down at once:
'Ctesippus, you can thank your lucky stars
you missed our guest – he ducked your blow, by god!
Else I would have planted my sharp spear in your bowels –
your father would have been busy with your funeral,
not your wedding here. Enough.
Don't let me see more offenses in my house,
not from anyone! I'm alive to it all, now,
the good and the bad – the boy you knew is gone.
But I still must bear with this, this lovely sight . . .
sheepflocks butchered, wine swilled, food squandered –
how can a man fight off so many single-handed?
But no more of your crimes against me, please!
Unless you're bent on cutting me down, now,
and I'd rather die, yes, better that by far
than have to look on at your outrage day by day:
guests treated to blows, men dragging the serving-women
through our noble house, exploiting them all, no shame!'

   Dead quiet. The suitors all fell silent, hushed.
At last Damastor's son Agelaus rose and said,
'Fair enough, my friends; when a man speaks well
we have no grounds for wrangling, no cause for abuse.
Hands off this stranger! Or any other servant
in King Odysseus' palace. But now a word
of friendly advice for Telemachus and his mother –

here's hoping it proves congenial to them both.
So long as your hearts still kept a spark alive
that Odysseus would return – that great, deep man –
who could blame you, playing the waiting game at home
and holding off the suitors? The better course, it's true.
What if Odysseus had returned, had made it home at last?
But now it's clear as day – the man will come no more.
So go, Telemachus, sit with your mother, coax her
to wed the best man here, the one who offers most,
so you can have and hold your father's estate,
eating and drinking here, your mind at peace
while mother plays the wife in another's house.'

   The young prince, keeping his poise, replied,
'I swear by Zeus, Agelaus, by all my father suffered –
dead, no doubt, or wandering far from Ithaca these days –
I don't delay my mother's marriage, not a moment,
I press her to wed the man who takes her heart.
I'll shower her myself with boundless gifts.
But I shrink from driving mother from our house,
issuing harsh commands against her will.
God forbid it ever comes to that!'
                    So he vowed
and Athena set off uncontrollable laughter in the suitors,
crazed them out of their minds – mad, hysterical laughter
seemed to break from the jaws of strangers, not their own,
and the meat they were eating oozed red with blood –
tears flooded their eyes, hearts possessed by grief.
The inspired seer Theoclymenus wailed out in their midst,
'Poor men, what terror is this that overwhelms you so?
Night shrouds your heads, your faces, down to your knees –

cries of mourning are bursting into fire – cheeks rivering
    tears –
the walls and the handsome crossbeams dripping dank with
    blood!
Ghosts, look, thronging the entrance, thronging the court,
go trooping down to the world of death and darkness!
The sun is blotted out of the sky – look there –
a lethal mist spreads all across the earth!'

                                    At that
they all broke into peals of laughter aimed at the seer –
Polybus' son Eurymachus braying first and foremost,
'Our guest just in from abroad, the man is raving!
Quick, my boys, hustle him out of the house,
into the meeting grounds, the light of day –
everything *here* he thinks is dark as night!'

   'Eurymachus,' the inspired prophet countered,
'when I want your escort, I'll ask for it myself.
I have eyes and ears, and both my feet, still,
and a head that's fairly sound,
nothing to be ashamed of. These will do
to take me past those doors . . .

                            Oh I can see it now –
the disaster closing on you all! There's no escaping it,
no way out – not for a single one of you suitors,
wild reckless fools, plotting outrage here,
the halls of Odysseus, great and strong as a god!'

   With that he marched out of the sturdy house
and went home to Piraeus, the host who warmed him in.
Now all the suitors, trading their snide glances, started

heckling Telemachus, made a mockery of his guests.
One or another brash young gallant scoffed,
'Telemachus, no one's more unlucky with his guests!'

'Look what your man dragged in – this mangy tramp
scraping for bread and wine!'
       'Not fit for good hard work,
the bag of bones –'
     'A useless dead weight on the land!'

'And then this charlatan up and apes the prophet.'

'Take it from me – you'll be better off by far –
toss your friends in a slave-ship –'
        'Pack them off
to Sicily, fast – they'll fetch you one sweet price!'

So they jeered, but the prince paid no attention . . .
silent, eyes riveted on his father, always waiting
the moment he'd lay hands on that outrageous mob.

And all the while Icarius' daughter, wise Penelope,
had placed her carved chair within earshot, at the door,
so she could catch each word they uttered in the hall.
Laughing rowdily, men prepared their noonday meal,
succulent, rich – they'd butchered quite a herd.
But as for supper, what could be less enticing
than what a goddess and a powerful man
would spread before them soon? A groaning feast –
for they'd been first to plot their vicious crimes.

4

Odysseus Strings His Bow

The time had come. The goddess Athena with her blazing
    eyes
inspired Penelope, Icarius' daughter, wary, poised,
to set the bow and the gleaming iron axes out
before her suitors waiting in Odysseus' hall –
to test their skill and bring their slaughter on.
Up the steep stairs to her room she climbed
and grasped in a steady hand the curved key –
fine bronze, with ivory haft attached –
and then with her chamber-women made her way
to a hidden storeroom, far in the palace depths,
and there they lay, the royal master's treasures:
bronze, gold and a wealth of hard wrought iron
and there it lay as well . . . his backsprung bow
with its quiver bristling arrows, shafts of pain.
Gifts from the old days, from a friend he'd met
in Lacedaemon – Iphitus, Eurytus' gallant son.
Once in Messene the two struck up together,
in sly Ortilochus' house, that time Odysseus
went to collect a debt the whole realm owed him,
for Messenian raiders had lifted flocks from Ithaca,
three hundred head in their oarswept ships, the herdsmen
    too.
So his father and island elders sent Odysseus off,
a young boy on a mission,

a distant embassy made to right that wrong.
Iphitus went there hunting the stock that *he* had lost,
a dozen mares still nursing their hardy suckling mules.
The same mares that would prove his certain death
when he reached the son of Zeus, that iron heart,
Heracles – the past master of monstrous works –
who killed the man, a guest in his own house.
Brutal. Not a care for the wrathful eyes of god
or rites of hospitality he had spread before him,
no, he dined him, then he murdered him, commandeered
those hard-hoofed mares for the hero's own grange.
Still on the trail of these when he met Odysseus,
Iphitus gave him the bow his father, mighty Eurytus,
used to wield as a young man, but when he died
in his lofty house he left it to his son.
In turn, Odysseus gave his friend a sharp sword
and a rugged spear to mark the start of friendship,
treasured ties that bind. But before they got to know
the warmth of each other's board, the son of Zeus
had murdered Iphitus, Eurytus' magnificent son
who gave the prince the bow.

                  That great weapon –
King Odysseus never took it abroad with him
when he sailed off to war in his long black ships.
He kept it stored away in his stately house,
guarding the memory of a cherished friend,
and only took that bow on hunts at home.

                           Now,
the lustrous queen soon reached the hidden vault
and stopped at the oaken doorsill, work an expert
sanded smooth and trued to the line some years ago,

planting the doorjambs snugly, hanging shining doors.
At once she loosed the thong from around its hook,
inserted the key and aiming straight and true,
shot back the bolts – and the rasping doors groaned
as loud as a bull will bellow, champing grass at pasture.
So as the key went home those handsome double doors
rang out now and sprang wide before her.
She stepped onto a plank where chests stood tall,
brimming with clothing scented sweet with cedar.
Reaching, tiptoe, lifting the bow down off its peg,
still secure in the burnished case that held it,
down she sank, laying the case across her knees,
and dissolved in tears with a high thin wail
as she drew her husband's weapon from its sheath . . .
Then, having wept and sobbed to her heart's content,
off she went to the hall to meet her proud admirers,
cradling her husband's backsprung bow in her arms,
its quiver bristling arrows, shafts of pain.
Her women followed, bringing a chest that held
the bronze and the iron axes, trophies won by the master.
That radiant woman, once she reached her suitors,
drawing her glistening veil across her cheeks,
paused now where a column propped the sturdy roof,
with one of her loyal handmaids stationed either side,
and delivered an ultimatum to her suitors:
'Listen to me, my overbearing friends!
You who plague this palace night and day,
drinking, eating us out of house and home
with the lord and master absent, gone so long –
the only excuse that you can offer is your zest
to win me as your bride. So, to arms, my gallants!

Here is the prize at issue, right before you, look –
I set before you the great bow of King Odysseus now!
The hand that can string this bow with greatest ease,
that shoots an arrow clean through all twelve axes –
he is the man I follow, yes, forsaking this house
where I was once a bride, this gracious house
so filled with the best that life can offer –
I shall always remember it, that I know . . .
even in my dreams.'

        She turned to Eumaeus,
ordered the good swineherd now to set the bow
and the gleaming iron axes out before the suitors.
He broke into tears as he received them, laid them down.
The cowherd wept too, when he saw his master's bow.
But Antinous wheeled on both and let them have it:
'Yokels, fools – you can't tell night from day!
You mawkish idiots, why are you sniveling here?
You're stirring up your mistress! Isn't she drowned
in grief already? She's lost her darling husband.
Sit down. Eat in peace, or take your snuffling
out of doors! But leave that bow right here –
our crucial test that makes or breaks us all.
No easy game, I wager, to string *his* polished bow.
Not a soul in the crowd can match Odysseus –
what a man he was . . .
I saw him once, remember him to this day,
though I was young and foolish way back then.'

        Smooth talk,
but deep in the suitor's heart his hopes were bent
on stringing the bow and shooting through the axes.
Antinous – fated to be the first man to taste

an arrow whipped from great Odysseus' hands,
the king he mocked, at ease in the king's house,
egging comrades on to mock him too.

                          'Amazing!'
Prince Telemachus waded in with a laugh:
'Zeus up there has robbed me of my wits.
My own dear mother, sensible as she is,
says she'll marry again, forsake our house,
and look at *me* – laughing for all I'm worth,
giggling like some fool. Step up, my friends!
Here is the prize at issue, right before you, look –
a woman who has no equal now in all Achaean country,
neither in holy Pylos, nor in Argos or Mycenae,
not even Ithaca itself or the loamy mainland.
You know it well. Why sing my mother's praises?
Come, let the games begin! No dodges, no delays,
no turning back from the stringing of the bow –
we'll see who wins, we will.
I'd even take a crack at the bow myself . . .
If I string it and shoot through all the axes,
I'd worry less if my noble mother left our house
with another man and left me here behind – man enough
at last to win my father's splendid prizes!'

                              With that
he leapt to his feet and dropped his bright-red cloak,
slipping the sword and sword-belt off his shoulders.
First he planted the axes, digging a long trench,
one for all, and trued them all to a line
then tamped the earth to bed them. Wonder took
the revelers looking on: his work so firm, precise,
though he'd never seen the axes ranged before.

64

He stood at the threshold, poised to try the bow . . .
Three times he made it shudder, straining to bend it,
three times his power flagged – but his hopes ran high
he'd string his father's bow and shoot through every iron
and now, struggling with all his might for the fourth time,
he would have strung the bow, but Odysseus shook his
    head
and stopped him short despite his tensing zeal.
'God help me,' the inspired prince cried out,
'must I be a weakling, a failure all my life?
Unless I'm just too young to trust my hands
to fight off any man who rises up against me.
Come, my betters, so much stronger than I am –
try the bow and finish off the contest.'

  He propped his father's weapon on the ground,
tilting it up against the polished well-hung doors
and resting a shaft aslant the bow's fine horn,
then back he went to the seat that he had left.
'Up, friends!' Antinous called, taking over.
'One man after another, left to right,
starting from where the steward pours the wine.'

  So Antinous urged and all agreed.
The first man up was Leodes, Oenops' son,
a seer who could see their futures in the smoke,
who always sat by the glowing winebowl, well back,
the one man in the group who loathed their reckless ways,
appalled by all their outrage. His turn first . . .
Picking up the weapon now and the swift arrow,
he stood at the threshold, poised to try the bow

but failed to bend it. As soon as he tugged the string
his hands went slack, his soft, uncallused hands,
and he called back to the suitors, 'Friends,
I can't bend it. Take it, someone – try.
Here is a bow to rob our best of life and breath,
all our best contenders! Still, better be dead
than live on here, never winning the prize
that tempts us all – forever in pursuit,
burning with expectation every day.
If there's still a suitor here who hopes,
who aches to marry Penelope, Odysseus' wife,
just let him try the bow; he'll see the truth!
He'll soon lay siege to another Argive woman
trailing her long robes, and shower her with gifts –
and then our queen can marry the one who offers most,
the man marked out by fate to be her husband.'

With those words he thrust the bow aside,
tilting it up against the polished well-hung doors
and resting a shaft aslant the bow's fine horn,
then back he went to the seat that he had left.
But Antinous turned on the seer, abuses flying:
'Leodes! what are you saying? what's got past your lips?
What awful, grisly nonsense – it shocks me to hear it –
"Here is a bow to rob our best of life and breath!"
Just because *you* can't string it, you're so weak?
Clearly your genteel mother never bred her boy
for the work of bending bows and shooting arrows.
We have champions in our ranks to string it quickly.
Hop to it, Melanthius!' – he barked at the goatherd –
'Rake the fire in the hall, pull up a big stool,

heap it with fleece and fetch that hefty ball
of lard from the stores inside. So we young lords
can heat and limber the bow and rub it down with grease
before we try again and finish off the contest!'

   The goatherd bustled about to rake the fire
still going strong. He pulled up a big stool,
heaped it with fleece and fetched the hefty ball
of lard from the stores inside. And the young men
limbered the bow, rubbing it down with hot grease,
then struggled to bend it back but failed. No use –
they fell far short of the strength the bow required.
Antinous still held off, dashing Eurymachus too,
the ringleaders of all the suitors,
head and shoulders and strongest of the lot.

                                    But now
the king's two men, the cowherd and the swineherd,
had slipped out of the palace side-by-side
and great Odysseus left the house to join them.
Once they were past the courtyard and the gates
he probed them deftly, surely: 'Cowherd, swineherd,
what, shall I blurt this out or keep it to myself?
No, speak out. The heart inside me says so.
How far would you go to fight beside Odysseus?
Say he dropped like *that* from a clear blue sky
and a god brought him back –
would you fight for the suitors or your king?
Tell me how you feel inside your hearts.'

   'Father Zeus,' the trusty cowherd shouted,
'bring my prayer to pass! Let the master come –

some god guide him now! You'd see my power,
my fighting arms in action!'

   Eumaeus echoed his prayer to all the gods
that their wise king would soon come home again.
Certain at least these two were loyal to the death,
Odysseus reassured them quickly: 'I'm right here,
here in the flesh – myself – and home at last,
after bearing twenty years of brutal hardship.
Now I know that of all my men you two alone
longed for my return. From the rest I've heard
not one real prayer that I come back again.
So now I'll tell you what's in store for *you*.
If a god beats down the lofty suitors at my hands,
I'll find you wives, both of you, grant you property,
sturdy houses beside my own, and in my eyes you'll be
comrades to Prince Telemachus, brothers from then on.
Come, I'll show you something – living proof –
know me for certain, put your minds at rest.

                          This scar,
look, where a boar's white tusk gored me, years ago,
hunting on Parnassus, Autolycus' sons and I.'

                               With that,
pushing back his rags, he revealed the great scar . . .
And the men gazed at it, scanned it, knew it well,
broke into tears and threw their arms around their
    master –
lost in affection, kissing his head and shoulders,
and so Odysseus kissed their heads and hands.
Now the sun would have set upon their tears
if Odysseus had not called a halt himself.

'No more weeping. Coming out of the house
a man might see us, tell the men inside.
Let's slip back in – singly, not in a pack.
I'll go first. You're next. Here's our signal.
When all the rest in there, our lordly friends,
are dead against my having the bow and quiver,
good Eumaeus, carry the weapon down the hall
and put it in my hands. Then tell the serving-women
to lock the snugly fitted doors to their own rooms.
If anyone hears from there the jolting blows
and groans of men, caught in our huge net,
not one of them show her face –
sit tight, keep to her weaving, not a sound.
You, my good Philoetius, here are your orders.
Shoot the bolt of the courtyard's outer gate,
lock it, lash it fast.'

                With that command
the master entered his well-constructed house
and back he went to the stool that he had left.
The king's two men, in turn, slipped in as well.

  Just now Eurymachus held the bow in his hands,
turning it over, tip to tip, before the blazing fire
to heat the weapon. But he failed to bend it even so
and the suitor's high heart groaned to bursting.
'A black day,' he exclaimed in wounded pride,
'a blow to myself, a blow to each man here!
It's less the marriage that mortifies me now –
that's galling too, but lots of women are left,
some in seagirt Ithaca, some in other cities.
What breaks my heart is the fact we fall so short

of great Odysseus' strength we cannot string his bow.
A disgrace to ring in the ears of men to come.'

'Eurymachus,' Eupithes' son Antinous countered,
'it will never come to that, as you well know.
Today is a feast-day up and down the island
in honor of the Archer God. Who flexes bows today?
Set it aside. Rest easy now. And all the axes,
let's just leave them planted where they are.
Trust me, no one's about to crash the gates
of Laertes' son and carry off these trophies.
Steward, pour some drops for the god in every cup,
we'll tip the wine, then put the bow to bed.
And first thing in the morning have Melanthius
bring the pick of his goats from all his herds
so we can burn the thighs to Apollo, god of archers –
then try the bow and finish off the contest.'

Welcome advice. And again they all agreed.
Heralds sprinkled water over their hands for rinsing,
the young men brimmed the mixing bowls with wine,
they tipped first drops for the god in every cup,
then poured full rounds for all. And now, once
they'd tipped libations out and drunk their fill,
the king of craft, Odysseus, said with all his cunning,
'Listen to me, you lords who court the noble queen.
I have to say what the heart inside me urges.
I appeal especially to Eurymachus, and you,
brilliant Antinous, who spoke so shrewdly now.
Give the bow a rest for today, leave it to the gods –
at dawn the Archer God will grant a victory

to the man he favours most.
                              For the moment,
give me the polished bow now, won't you? So,
to amuse you all, I can try my hand, my strength . . .
is the old force still alive inside these gnarled limbs?
Or has a life of roaming, years of rough neglect,
destroyed it long ago?'
                        Modest words
that sent them all into hot, indignant rage,
fearing he just might string the polished bow.
So Antinous rounded on him, dressed him down:
'Not a shred of sense in your head, you filthy drifter!
Not content to feast at your ease with us, the island's pride?
Never denied your full share of the banquet, never,
you can listen in on our secrets. No one else
can eavesdrop on our talk, no tramp, no beggar.
The wine has overpowered you, heady wine –
the ruin of many another man, whoever
gulps it down and drinks beyond his limit.
Wine – it drove the Centaur, famous Eurytion,
mad in the halls of lionhearted Pirithous.
There to visit the Lapiths, crazed with wine
the headlong Centaur bent to his ugly work
in the prince's own house! His hosts sprang up,
seized with fury, dragged him across the forecourt,
flung him out of doors, hacking his nose and ears off
with their knives, no mercy. The creature reeled away,
still blind with drink, his heart like a wild storm,
loaded with all the frenzy in his mind!
                                        And so
the feud between mortal men and Centaurs had its start.

But the drunk was first to bring disaster on himself
by drowning in his cups. You too, I promise you
no end of trouble if you should string that bow.
You'll meet no kindness in our part of the world –
we'll sail you off in a black ship to Echetus,
the mainland king who wrecks all men alive.
Nothing can save you from his royal grip!
So drink, but hold your peace,
don't take on the younger, stronger men.'

   'Antinous,' watchful Penelope stepped in,
'how impolite it would be, how wrong, to scant
whatever guest Telemachus welcomes to his house.
You really think – if the stranger trusts so to his hands
and strength that he strings Odysseus' great bow –
he'll take me home and claim me as his bride?
He never dreamed of such a thing, I'm sure.
Don't let that ruin the feast for any reveler here.
Unthinkable – nothing, nothing could be worse.'

   Polybus' son Eurymachus had an answer:
'Wise Penelope, daughter of Icarius, do we really
expect the man to wed you? Unthinkable, I know.
But we do recoil at the talk of men and women.
One of the island's meaner sort will mutter,
"Look at the riffraff courting a king's wife.
Weaklings, look, they can't even string his bow.
But along came this beggar, drifting out of the blue –
strung his bow with ease and shot through all the axes!"
Gossip will fly. We'll hang our heads in shame.'

'Shame?' alert Penelope protested –
'How can you hope for any public fame at all?
You who disgrace, devour a great man's house and home!
Why hang your heads in shame over next to nothing?
Our friend here is a strapping, well-built man
and claims to be the son of a noble father.
Come, hand him the bow now, let's just see . . .
I tell you this – and I'll make good my word –
if he strings the bow and Apollo grants him glory,
I'll dress him in shirt and cloak, in handsome clothes,
I'll give him a good sharp lance to fight off men and dogs,
give him a two-edged sword and sandals for his feet
and send him off, wherever his heart desires.'

                                        'Mother,'
poised Telemachus broke in now, 'my father's bow –
no Achaean on earth has more right than I
to give it or withhold it, as I please.
Of all the lords in Ithaca's rocky heights
or the islands facing Elis grazed by horses,
not a single one will force or thwart my will,
even if I decide to give our guest this bow –
a gift outright – to carry off himself.

                                So, mother,
go back to your quarters. Tend to your own tasks,
the distaff and the loom, and keep the women
working hard as well. As for the bow now,
men will see to that, but I most of all:
I hold the reins of power in this house.'

                                        Astonished,
she withdrew to her own room. She took to heart
the clear good sense in what her son had said.

73

Climbing up to the lofty chamber with her women,
she fell to weeping for Odysseus, her beloved husband,
till watchful Athena sealed her eyes with welcome sleep.

And now the loyal swineherd had lifted up the bow,
was taking it toward the king, when all the suitors
burst out in an ugly uproar through the palace –
brash young bullies, this or that one heckling,
'Where on earth are you going with that bow?'

'You, you grubby swineherd, are you crazy?'

'The speedy dogs you reared will eat your corpse –'

'Out there with your pigs, out in the cold, alone!'

'If only Apollo and all the gods shine down on us!'

Eumaeus froze in his tracks, put down the bow,
panicked by every outcry in the hall.
Telemachus shouted too, from the other side,
and full of threats: 'Carry on with the bow, old boy!
If you serve too many masters, you'll soon suffer.
Look sharp, or I'll pelt you back to your farm
with flying rocks. I may be younger than you
but I'm much stronger. If only I had that edge
in fists and brawn over all this courting crowd,
I'd soon dispatch them – licking their wounds at last –
clear of our palace where they plot their vicious plots!'

His outburst sent them all into gales of laughter,
blithe and oblivious, that dissolved their pique
against the prince. The swineherd took the bow,
carried it down the hall to his ready, waiting king
and standing by him, placed it in his hands,
then he called the nurse aside and whispered,
'Good Eurycleia – Telemachus commands you now
to lock the snugly fitted doors to your own rooms.
If anyone hears from there the jolting blows
and groans of men, caught in our huge net,
not one of you show your face –
sit tight, keep to your weaving, not a sound.'

  That silenced the old nurse –
she barred the doors that led from the long hall.
The cowherd quietly bounded out of the house
to lock the gates of the high-stockaded court.
Under the portico lay a cable, ship's tough gear:
he lashed the gates with this, then slipped back in
and ran and sat on the stool that he'd just left,
eyes riveted on Odysseus.
                    Now *he* held the bow
in his own hands, turning it over, tip to tip,
testing it, this way, that way . . . fearing worms
had bored through the weapon's horn with the master gone
    abroad.
A suitor would glance at his neighbor, jeering, taunting,
'Look at our connoisseur of bows!'
                        'Sly old fox –
maybe he's got bows like it, stored in *his* house.'

'That or he's bent on making one himself.'

'Look how he twists and turns it in his hands!'

'The clever tramp means trouble –'

'I wish him luck,' some cocksure lord chimed in,
'as good as his luck in bending back that weapon!'

So they mocked, but Odysseus, mastermind in action,
once he'd handled the great bow and scanned every inch,
then, like an expert singer skilled at lyre and song –
who strains a string to a new peg with ease,
making the pliant sheep-gut fast at either end –
so with his virtuoso ease Odysseus strung his mighty bow.
Quickly his right hand plucked the string to test its pitch
and under his touch it sang out clear and sharp as a
    swallow's cry.
Horror swept through the suitors, faces blanching white,
and Zeus cracked the sky with a bolt, his blazing sign,
and the great man who had borne so much rejoiced at last
that the son of cunning Cronus flung that omen down for
    him.
He snatched a winged arrow lying bare on the board –
the rest still bristled deep inside the quiver,
soon to be tasted by all the feasters there.
Setting shaft on the handgrip, drawing the notch
and bowstring back, back . . . right from his stool,
just as he sat but aiming straight and true, he let fly –
and never missing an ax from the first ax-handle
clean on through to the last and out

the shaft with its weighted brazen head shot free!

'Telemachus,'
    Odysseus looked to his son and said, 'your guest,
sitting here in your house, has not disgraced you.
No missing the mark, look, and no long labor spent
to string the bow. My strength's not broken yet,
not quite so frail as the mocking suitors thought.
But the hour has come to serve our masters right –
supper in broad daylight – then to other revels,
song and dancing, all that crowns a feast.'

    He paused with a warning nod, and at that sign
Prince Telemachus, son of King Odysseus,
girding his sharp sword on, clamping hand to spear,
took his stand by a chair that flanked his father –
his bronze spearpoint glinting now like fire . . .

5

Slaughter in the Hall

Now stripping back his rags Odysseus master of craft and
    battle
vaulted onto the great threshold, gripping his bow and
    quiver
bristling arrows, and poured his flashing shafts before him,
loose at his feet, and thundered out to all the suitors:
'Look – your crucial test is finished, now, at last!
But another target's left that no one's hit before –
we'll see if *I* can hit it – Apollo give me glory!'

With that he trained a stabbing arrow on Antinous . . .
just lifting a gorgeous golden loving-cup in his hands,
just tilting the two-handled goblet back to his lips,
about to drain the wine – and slaughter the last thing
on the suitor's mind: who could dream that one foe
in that crowd of feasters, however great his power,
would bring down death on himself, and black doom?
But Odysseus aimed and shot Antinous square in the throat
and the point went stabbing clean through the soft neck and
    out –
and off to the side he pitched, the cup dropped from his grasp
as the shaft sank home, and the man's life-blood came spurting
from his nostrils –

               thick red jets –

                      a sudden thrust of his foot –

he kicked away the table –
                                food showered across the floor,
the bread and meats soaked in a swirl of bloody filth.
The suitors burst into uproar all throughout the house
when they saw their leader down. They leapt from their
    seats,
milling about, desperate, scanning the stone walls –
not a shield in sight, no rugged spear to seize.
They wheeled on Odysseus, lashing out in fury:
'Stranger, shooting at men will cost your life!'

'Your game is over – you, you've shot your last!'

'You'll never escape your own headlong death!'

'You killed the best in Ithaca – our fine prince!'

'Vultures will eat your corpse!'
                                Groping, frantic –
each one persuading himself the guest had killed
the man by chance. Poor fools, blind to the fact
that all their necks were in the noose, their doom sealed.
With a dark look, the wily fighter Odysseus shouted back,
'You dogs! you never imagined I'd return from Troy –
so cocksure that you bled my house to death,
ravished my serving-women – wooed my wife
behind my back while I was still alive!
No fear of the gods who rule the skies up there,
no fear that men's revenge might arrive someday –
now all your necks are in the noose – your doom is sealed!'

Terror gripped them all, blanched their faces white,
each man glancing wildly – how to escape his instant death?
Only Eurymachus had the breath to venture, 'If you,
you're truly Odysseus of Ithaca, home at last,
you're right to accuse these men of what they've done –
so much reckless outrage here in your palace,
so much on your lands. But here he lies,
quite dead, and he incited it all – Antinous –
look, the man who drove us all to crime!
Not that he needed marriage, craved it so;
he'd bigger game in mind – though Zeus barred his way –
he'd lord it over Ithaca's handsome country, king himself,
once he'd lain in wait for your son and cut him down!
But now he's received the death that he deserved.
So spare your own people! Later we'll recoup
your costs with a tax laid down upon the land,
covering all we ate and drank inside your halls,
and each of us here will pay full measure too –
twenty oxen in value, bronze and gold we'll give
until we melt your heart. Before we've settled,
who on earth could blame you for your rage?'

But the battle-master kept on glaring, seething.
'No, Eurymachus! Not if you paid me all your father's wealth –
all you possess now, and all that could pour in from the
        world's end –
no, not even then would I stay my hands from slaughter
till all you suitors had paid for all your crimes!
Now life or death – your choice – fight me or flee
if you hope to escape your sudden bloody doom!
I doubt one man in the lot will save his skin!'

His menace shook their knees, their hearts too
but Eurymachus spoke again, now to the suitors: 'Friends!
This man will never restrain his hands, invincible hands –
now that he's seized that polished bow and quiver, look,
he'll shoot from the sill until he's killed us all!
So fight – call up the joy of battle! Swords out!
Tables lifted – block his arrows winging death!
Charge him, charge in a pack –
try to rout the man from the sill, the doors,
race through town and sound an alarm at once –
our friend would soon see he's shot his bolt!'

                                        Brave talk –
he drew his two-edged sword, bronze, honed for the kill
and hurled himself at the king with a raw savage cry
in the same breath that Odysseus loosed an arrow
ripping his breast beside the nipple so hard
it lodged in the man's liver –
out of his grasp the sword dropped to the ground –
over his table, head over heels he tumbled, doubled up,
flinging his food and his two-handled cup across the floor –
he smashed the ground with his forehead, writhing in pain,
both feet flailing out, and his high seat tottered –
the mist of death came swirling down his eyes.

Amphinomus rushed the king in all his glory,
charging him face-to-face, a slashing sword drawn –
if only he could force him clear of the doorway, now,
but Telemachus – too quick – stabbed the man from behind,
plunging his bronze spear between the suitor's shoulders
and straight on through his chest the point came jutting
    out –

down he went with a thud, his forehead slammed the
    ground.
Telemachus swerved aside, leaving his long spearshaft
lodged in Amphinomus – fearing some suitor just might
lunge in from behind as he tugged the shaft,
impale him with a sword or hack him down,
crouching over the corpse.
He went on the run, reached his father at once
and halting right beside him, let fly, 'Father –
now I'll get you a shield and a pair of spears,
a helmet of solid bronze to fit your temples!
I'll arm myself on the way back and hand out
arms to the swineherd, arm the cowherd too –
we'd better fight equipped!'

                  'Run, fetch them,'
the wily captain urged, 'while I've got arrows left
to defend me – or they'll force me from the doors
while I fight on alone!'

    Telemachus moved to his father's orders smartly.
Off he ran to the room where the famous arms lay stored,
took up four shields, eight spears, four bronze helmets
ridged with horsehair crests and, loaded with these,
ran back to reach his father's side in no time.
The prince was first to case himself in bronze
and his servants followed suit – both harnessed up
and all three flanked Odysseus, mastermind of war,
and he, as long as he'd arrows left to defend himself,
kept picking suitors off in the palace, one by one
and down they went, corpse on corpse in droves.
Then, when the royal archer's shafts ran out,

82

he leaned his bow on a post of the massive doors –
where walls of the hallway catch the light – and armed:
across his shoulder he slung a buckler four plies thick,
over his powerful head he set a well-forged helmet,
the horsehair crest atop it tossing, bristling terror,
and grasped two rugged lances tipped with fiery bronze.

Now a side-door was fitted into the main wall –
right at the edge of the great hall's stone sill –
and led to a passage always shut by good tight boards.
But Odysseus gave the swineherd strict commands
to stand hard by the side-door, guard it well –
the only way the suitors might break out.
Agelaus called to his comrades with a plan:
'Friends, can't someone climb through the hatch? –
tell men outside to sound the alarm, be quick –
our guest would soon see he'd shot his last!'

The goatherd Melanthius answered, 'Not a chance,
my lord – the door to the courtyard's much too near,
dangerous too, the mouth of the passage cramped.
One strong man could block us, one and all!
No, I'll fetch you some armor to harness on,
out of the storeroom – there, nowhere else, I'm sure,
the king and his gallant son have stowed their arms!'

With that the goatherd clambered up through smoke-
      ducts
high on the wall and scurried into Odysseus' storeroom,
bundled a dozen shields, as many spears and helmets
ridged with horsehair crests and, loaded with these,

rushed back down to the suitors, quickly issued arms.
Odysseus' knees shook, his heart too, when he saw them
buckling on their armor, brandishing long spears –
here was a battle looming, well he knew.
He turned at once to Telemachus, warnings flying:
'A bad break in the fight, my boy! One of the women's
tipped the odds against us – or could it be the goatherd?'

'My fault, father,' the cool clear prince replied,
'the blame's all mine. That snug door to the vault,
I left it ajar – they've kept a better watch than I.
Go, Eumaeus, shut the door to the storeroom,
check and see if it's one of the women's tricks
or Dolius' son Melanthius. He's our man, I'd say.'

And even as they conspired, back the goatherd
climbed to the room to fetch more burnished arms,
but Eumaeus spotted him, quickly told his king
who stood close by: 'Odysseus, wily captain,
there he goes again, the infernal nuisance –
just as we suspected – back to the storeroom.
Give me a clear command!
Do I kill the man – if I can take him down –
or drag him back to you, here, to pay in full
for the vicious work he's plotted in your house?'

Odysseus, master of tactics, answered briskly,
'I and the prince will keep these brazen suitors
crammed in the hall, for all their battle-fury.
You two wrench Melanthius' arms and legs behind him,
fling him down in the storeroom – lash his back to a plank

and strap a twisted cable fast to the scoundrel's body,
hoist him up a column until he hits the rafters –
let him dangle in agony, still alive,
for a good long time!'

    They hung on his orders, keen to do his will.
Off they ran to the storeroom, unseen by him inside –
Melanthius, rummaging after arms, deep in a dark recess
as the two men took their stand, either side of the doorposts,
poised till the goatherd tried to cross the doorsill . . .
one hand clutching a crested helmet, the other
an ample old buckler blotched with mildew,
the shield Laertes bore as a young soldier once
but there it lay for ages, seams on the handstraps split –
Quick, they rushed him, seized him, haled him back by the
        hair,
flung him down on the floor, writhing with terror, bound him
hand and foot with a chafing cord, wrenched his limbs
back, back till the joints locked tight –
just as Laertes' cunning son commanded –
they strapped a twisted cable round his body,
hoisted him up a column until he hit the rafters,
then you mocked him, Eumaeus, my good swineherd:
'Now stand guard through the whole night, Melanthius –
stretched out on a soft bed fit for *you*, your highness!
You're bound to see the Morning rising up from the Ocean,
mounting her golden throne – at just the hour you always
drive in goats to feast the suitors in the hall!'

    So they left him, trussed in his agonizing sling;
they clapped on armor again, shut the gleaming doors

and ran to rejoin Odysseus, mastermind of war.
And now as the ranks squared off, breathing fury –
four at the sill confronting a larger, stronger force
arrayed inside the hall – now Zeus's daughter Athena,
taking the build and voice of Mentor, swept in
and Odysseus, thrilled to see her, cried out,
'Rescue us, Mentor, now it's life or death!
Remember your old comrade – all the service
I offered you! We were boys together!'

                              So he cried
yet knew in his bones it was Athena, Driver of Armies.
But across the hall the suitors brayed against her,
Agelaus first, his outburst full of threats:
'Mentor, never let Odysseus trick you into
siding with *him* to fight against the suitors.
Here's our plan of action, and we will see it through!
Once we've killed them both, the father and the son,
we'll kill you too, for all you're bent on doing
here in the halls – you'll pay with your own head!
And once our swords have stopped your violence cold –
all your property, all in your house, your fields,
we'll lump it all with Odysseus' rich estate
and never let your sons live on in your halls
or free your wife and daughters to walk through town!'

Naked threats – and Athena hit new heights of rage,
she lashed out at Odysseus now with blazing accusations:
'Where's it gone, Odysseus – your power, your fighting heart?
The great soldier who fought for famous white-armed Helen,
battling Trojans nine long years – nonstop, no mercy,
mowing their armies down in grueling battle –

you who seized the broad streets of Troy
with your fine strategic stroke! How can you –
now you've returned to your own house, your own wealth –
bewail the loss of your combat strength in a war with *suitors*?
Come, old friend, stand by me! You'll see action now,
see how Mentor the son of Alcimus, that brave fighter,
kills your enemies, pays you back for service!'
                                        Rousing words –
but she gave no all-out turning of the tide, not yet,
she kept on testing Odysseus and his gallant son,
putting their force and fighting heart to proof.
For all the world like a swallow in their sight
she flew on high to perch
on the great hall's central roofbeam black with smoke.

   But the suitors closed ranks, commanded now by
       Damastor's son
Agelaus, flanked by Eurynomus, Demoptolemus and
       Amphimedon,
Pisander, Polyctor's son, and Polybus ready, waiting –
head and shoulders the best and bravest of the lot
still left to fight for their lives,
now that the pelting shafts had killed the rest.
Agelaus spurred his comrades on with battle-plans:
'Friends, at last the man's invincible hands are useless!
Mentor has mouthed some empty boasts and flitted off –
just four are left to fight at the front doors. So now,
no wasting your long spears – all at a single hurl,
just six of us launch out in the first wave!
If Zeus is willing, we may hit Odysseus,
carry off the glory! The rest are nothing

once the captain's down!'
                                    At his command,
concentrating their shots, all six hurled as one
but Athena sent the whole salvo wide of the mark –
one of them hit the jamb of the great hall's doors,
another the massive door itself, and the heavy bronze point
of a third ashen javelin crashed against the wall.
Seeing his men untouched by the suitors' flurry,
steady Odysseus leapt to take command:
'Friends! now it's for *us* to hurl at them, I say,
into this ruck of suitors! Topping all their crimes
they're mad to strip the armor off our bodies!'

Taking aim at the ranks, all four let fly as one
and the lances struck home – Odysseus killed Demoptolemus,
Telemachus killed Euryades – the swineherd, Elatus –
and the cowherd cut Pisander down in blood.
They bit the dust of the broad floor, all as one.
Back to the great hall's far recess the others shrank
as the four rushed in and plucked up spears from corpses.

And again the suitors hurled their whetted shafts
but Athena sent the better part of the salvo wide –
one of them hit the jamb of the great hall's doors,
another the massive door itself, and the heavy bronze point
of a third ashen javelin crashed against the wall.
True, Amphimedon nicked Telemachus on the wrist –
the glancing blade just barely broke his skin.
Ctesippus sent a long spear sailing over
Eumaeus' buckler, grazing his shoulder blade
but the weapon skittered off and hit the ground.

And again those led by the brilliant battle-master
hurled their razor spears at the suitors' ranks –
and now Odysseus raider of cities hit Eurydamas,
Telemachus hit Amphimedon – Eumaeus, Polybus –
and the cowherd stabbed Ctesippus
right in the man's chest and triumphed over his body:
'Love your mockery, do you? Son of that blowhard
    Polytherses!
No more shooting off your mouth, you idiot, such big talk –
leave the last word to the gods – they're much stronger!
Take this spear, this guest-gift, for the cow's hoof
you once gave King Odysseus begging in his house!'

  So the master of longhorn cattle had his say –
as Odysseus, fighting at close quarters, ran Agelaus
through with a long lance – Telemachus speared Leocritus
so deep in the groin the bronze came punching out his back
and the man crashed headfirst, slamming the ground full-
    face.
And now Athena, looming out of the rafters high above
    them,
brandished her man-destroying shield of thunder, terrifying
the suitors out of their minds, and down the hall they
    panicked –
wild, like herds stampeding, driven mad as the darting gadfly
strikes in the late spring when the long days come round.
The attackers struck like eagles, crook-clawed, hook-beaked,
swooping down from a mountain ridge to harry smaller
    birds
that skim across the flatland, cringing under the clouds
but the eagles plunge in fury, rip their lives out – hopeless,

never a chance of flight or rescue – and people love the sport –
so the attackers routed suitors headlong down the hall,
wheeling into the slaughter, slashing left and right
and grisly screams broke from skulls cracked open –
the whole floor awash with blood.

                          Leodes now –
he flung himself at Odysseus, clutched his knees,
crying out to the king with a sudden, winging prayer:
'I hug your knees, Odysseus – mercy! spare my life!
Never, I swear, did I harass any woman in your house –
never a word, a gesture – nothing, no, I tried
to restrain the suitors, whoever did such things.
They wouldn't listen, keep their hands to themselves –
so reckless, so they earn their shameful fate.
But I was just their prophet –
my hands are clean – and I'm to die their death!
Look at the thanks I get for years of service!'

    A killing look, and the wry soldier answered,
'Only a priest, a prophet for this mob, you say?
How hard you must have prayed in my own house
that the heady day of my return would never dawn –
my dear wife would be yours, would bear your children!
For that there's no escape from grueling death – you die!'

    And snatching up in one powerful hand a sword
left on the ground – Agelaus dropped it when he fell –
Odysseus hacked the prophet square across the neck
and the praying head went tumbling in the dust.

                          Now one was left,
trying still to escape black death. Phemius, Terpis' son,

the bard who always performed among the suitors –
they forced the man to sing . . .
There he stood, backing into the side-door,
still clutching his ringing lyre in his hands,
his mind in turmoil, torn – what should he do?
Steal from the hall and crouch at the altar-stone
of Zeus who Guards the Court, where time and again
Odysseus and Laertes burned the long thighs of oxen?
Or throw himself on the master's mercy, clasp his knees?
That was the better way – or so it struck him, yes,
grasp the knees of Laertes' royal son. And so,
cradling his hollow lyre, he laid it on the ground
between the mixing-bowl and the silver-studded throne,
then rushed up to Odysseus, yes, and clutched his knees,
singing out to his king with a stirring, winged prayer:
'I hug your knees, Odysseus – mercy! spare my life!
What a grief it will be to you for all the years to come
if you kill the singer now, who sings for gods and men.
I taught myself the craft, but a god has planted
deep in my spirit all the paths of song –
songs I'm fit to sing for you as for a god.
Calm your bloodlust now – don't take my head!
He'd bear me out, your own dear son Telemachus –
never of *my* own will, never for any gain did I
perform in your house, singing after the suitors
had their feasts. They were too strong, too many –
they forced me to come and sing – I had no choice!'

   The inspired Prince Telemachus heard his pleas
and quickly said to his father close beside him,
'Stop, don't cut him down! This one's innocent.

So is the herald Medon – the one who always
tended me in the house when I was little –
spare him too. Unless he's dead by now,
killed by Philoetius or Eumaeus here –
or ran into *you* rampaging through the halls.'

    The herald pricked up his anxious ears at that . . .
cautious soul, he cowered, trembling, under a chair –
wrapped in an oxhide freshly stripped – to dodge black
       death.
He jumped in a flash from there, threw off the smelly hide
and scuttling up to Telemachus, clutching his knees,
the herald begged for life in words that fluttered:
'Here I am, dear boy – spare me! Tell your father,
flushed with victory, not to kill me with his sword –
enraged as he is with these young lords who bled
his palace white and showed you no respect,
the reckless fools!'
                    Breaking into a smile
the canny Odysseus reassured him, 'Courage!
The prince has pulled you through, he's saved you now
so you can take it to heart and tell the next man too:
clearly doing good puts doing bad to shame.
Now leave the palace, go and sit outside –
out in the courtyard, clear of the slaughter –
you and the bard with all his many songs.
Wait till I've done some household chores
that call for my attention.'

    The two men scurried out of the house at once
and crouched at the altar-stone of mighty Zeus –

glancing left and right,
fearing death would strike at any moment.

   Odysseus scanned his house to see if any man
still skulked alive, still hoped to avoid black death.
But he found them one and all in blood and dust . . .
great hauls of them down and out like fish that fishermen
drag from the churning gray surf in looped and coiling nets
and fling ashore on a sweeping hook of beach – some noble
     catch
heaped on the sand, twitching, lusting for fresh salt sea
but the Sungod hammers down and burns their lives out . . .
so the suitors lay in heaps, corpse covering corpse.
At last the seasoned fighter turned to his son:
'Telemachus, go, call the old nurse here –
I must tell her all that's on my mind.'

Telemachus ran to do his father's bidding,
shook the women's doors, calling Eurycleia:
'Come out now! Up with you, good old woman!
You who watch over all the household hands –
quick, my father wants you, needs to have a word!'

   Crisp command that left the old nurse hushed –
she spread the doors to the well-constructed hall,
slipped out in haste, and the prince led her on . . .
She found Odysseus in the thick of slaughtered corpses,
splattered with bloody filth like a lion that's devoured
some ox of the field and lopes home, covered with blood,
his chest streaked, both jaws glistening, dripping red –
a sight to strike terror. So Odysseus looked now,

splattered with gore, his thighs, his fighting hands,
and she, when she saw the corpses, all the pooling blood,
was about to lift a cry of triumph – here was a great exploit,
look – but the soldier held her back and checked her zeal
with warnings winging home: 'Rejoice in your heart,
old woman – peace! No cries of triumph now.
It's unholy to glory over the bodies of the dead.
These men the doom of the gods has brought low,
and their own indecent acts. They'd no regard
for any man on earth – good or bad –
who chanced to come their way. And so, thanks
to their reckless work, they met this shameful fate.
Quick, report in full on the women in my halls –
who are disloyal to me, who are guiltless?'

                                    'Surely, child,'
his fond old nurse replied, 'now here's the truth.
Fifty women you have inside your house,
women we've trained to do their duties well,
to card the wool and bear the yoke of service.
Some dozen in all went tramping to their shame,
thumbing their noses at me, at the queen herself!
And Telemachus, just now come of age – his mother
would never let the boy take charge of the maids.
But let me climb to her well-lit room upstairs
and tell your wife the news –
some god has put the woman fast asleep.'

  'Don't wake her yet,' the crafty man returned,
'you tell those women to hurry here at once –
just the ones who've shamed us all along.'

Away the old nurse bustled through the house
to give the women orders, rush them to the king.
Odysseus called Telemachus over, both herdsmen too,
with strict commands: 'Start clearing away the bodies.
Make the women pitch in too. Chairs and tables –
scrub them down with sponges, rinse them clean.
And once you've put the entire house in order,
march the women out of the great hall – between
the roundhouse and the courtyard's strong stockade –
and hack them with your swords, slash out all their lives –
blot out of their minds the joys of love they relished
under the suitors' bodies, rutting on the sly!'

The women crowded in, huddling all together . . .
wailing convulsively, streaming live warm tears.
First they carried out the bodies of the dead
and propped them under the courtyard colonnade,
standing them one against another. Odysseus
shouted commands himself, moving things along
and they kept bearing out the bodies – they were forced.
Next they scrubbed down the elegant chairs and tables,
washed them with sopping sponges, rinsed them clean.
Then Telemachus and the herdsmen scraped smooth
the packed earth floor of the royal house with spades
as the women gathered up the filth and piled it outside.
And then, at last, once the entire house was put in order,
they marched the women out of the great hall – between
the roundhouse and the courtyard's strong stockade –
crammed them into a dead end, no way out from there,
and stern Telemachus gave the men their orders:
'No clean death for the likes of them, by god!

Not from me – they showered abuse on my head,
my mother's too!
                    'You sluts – the suitors' whores!'

   With that, taking a cable used on a dark-prowed ship
he coiled it over the roundhouse, lashed it fast to a tall column,
hoisting it up so high no toes could touch the ground.
Then, as doves or thrushes beating their spread wings
against some snare rigged up in thickets – flying in
for a cozy nest but a grisly bed receives them –
so the women's heads were trapped in a line,
nooses yanking their necks up, one by one
so all might die a pitiful, ghastly death . . .
they kicked up heels for a little – not for long.
                                        Melanthius?
They hauled him out through the doorway, into the court,
lopped his nose and ears with a ruthless knife,
tore his genitals out for the dogs to eat raw
and in manic fury hacked off hands and feet.
                                        Then,
once they'd washed their own hands and feet,
they went inside again to join Odysseus.
Their work was done with now.
But the king turned to devoted Eurycleia, saying,
'Bring sulfur, nurse, to scour all this pollution –
bring me fire too, so I can fumigate the house.
And call Penelope here with all her women –
tell all the maids to come back in at once.'

   'Well said, my boy,' his old nurse replied,
'right to the point. But wait,

let me fetch you a shirt and cloak to wrap you.
No more dawdling round the palace, nothing but rags
to cover those broad shoulders – it's a scandal!'

'Fire first,' the good soldier answered.
'Light me a fire to purify this house.'

The devoted nurse snapped to his command,
brought her master fire and brimstone. Odysseus
purged his palace, halls and court, with cleansing fumes.

Then back through the royal house the old nurse went
to tell the women the news and bring them in at once.
They came crowding out of their quarters, torch in hand,
flung their arms around Odysseus, hugged him, home at last,
and kissed his head and shoulders, seized his hands, and he,
overcome by a lovely longing, broke down and wept . . .
deep in his heart he knew them one and all.

6

The Great Rooted Bed

Up to the rooms the old nurse clambered, chuckling all the
    way,
to tell the queen her husband was here now, home at last.
Her knees bustling, feet shuffling over each other,
till hovering at her mistress' head she spoke:
'Penelope – child – wake up and see for yourself,
with your own eyes, all you dreamed of, all your days!
He's here – Odysseus – he's come home, at long last!
He's killed the suitors, swaggering young brutes
who plagued his house, wolfed his cattle down,
rode roughshod over his son!'

   'Dear old nurse,' wary Penelope replied,
'the gods have made you mad. They have that power,
putting lunacy into the clearest head around
or setting a half-wit on the path to sense.
They've unhinged you, and you were once so sane.
Why do you mock me? – haven't I wept enough? –
telling such wild stories, interrupting my sleep,
sweet sleep that held me, sealed my eyes just now.
Not once have I slept so soundly since the day
Odysseus sailed away to see that cursed city . . .
Destroy, I call it – I hate to say its name!
Now down you go. Back to your own quarters.
If any other woman of mine had come to me,

rousing me out of sleep with such a tale,
I'd have her bundled back to her room in pain.
It's only your old gray head that spares you that!'

'Never' – the fond old nurse kept pressing on –
'dear child, I'd never mock you! No, it's all true,
he's here – Odysseus – he's come home, just as I tell you!
He's the stranger they all manhandled in the hall.
Telemachus knew he was here, for days and days,
but he knew enough to hide his father's plans
so *he* could pay those vipers back in kind!'

Penelope's heart burst in joy, she leapt from bed,
her eyes streaming tears, she hugged the old nurse
and cried out with an eager, winging word,
'Please, dear one, give me the whole story.
If he's really home again, just as you tell me,
how did he get those shameless suitors in his clutches? –
single-handed, braving an army always camped inside.'

'I have no idea,' the devoted nurse replied.
'I didn't see it, I didn't ask – all I heard
was the choking groans of men cut down in blood.
We crouched in terror – a dark nook of our quarters –
all of us locked tight behind those snug doors
till your boy Telemachus came and called me out –
his father rushed him there to do just that. And then
I found Odysseus in the thick of slaughtered corpses;
there he stood and all around him, over the beaten floor,
the bodies sprawled in heaps, lying one on another . . .
How it would have thrilled your heart to see him –

splattered with bloody filth, a lion with his kill!
And now they're all stacked at the courtyard gates –
he's lit a roaring fire,
he's purifying the house with cleansing fumes
and he's sent me here to bring you back to him.
Follow me down! So now, after all the years of grief,
you two can embark, loving hearts, along the road to joy.
Look, your dreams, put off so long, come true at last –
he's back alive, home at his hearth, and found you,
found his son still here. And all those suitors
who did him wrong, he's paid them back, he has,
right in his own house!'

                    'Hush, dear woman,'
guarded Penelope cautioned her at once.
'Don't laugh, don't cry in triumph – not yet.
You know how welcome the sight of him would be
to all in the house, and to me most of all
and the son we bore together.
But the story can't be true, not as you tell it,
no, it must be a god who's killed our brazen friends –
up in arms at their outrage, heartbreaking crimes.
They'd no regard for any man on earth –
good or bad – who chanced to come their way. So,
thanks to their reckless work they die their deaths.
Odysseus? Far from Achaea now, he's lost all hope
of coming home . . . he's lost and gone himself.'

   'Child,' the devoted old nurse protested,
'what nonsense you let slip through your teeth.
Here's your husband, warming his hands at his own hearth,
here – and you, you say he'll never come home again,

always the soul of trust! All right, this too –
I'll give you a sign, a proof that's plain as day.
That scar, made years ago by a boar's white tusk –
I spotted the scar myself, when I washed his feet,
and I tried to tell you, ah, but he, the crafty rascal,
clamped his hand on my mouth – I couldn't say a word.
Follow me down now. I'll stake my life on it:
if I am lying to *you* –
kill me with a thousand knives of pain!'

   'Dear old nurse,' composed Penelope responded,
'deep as you are, my friend, you'll find it hard
to plumb the plans of the everlasting gods.
All the same, let's go and join my son
so I can see the suitors lying dead
and see . . . the one who killed them.'

                        With that thought
Penelope started down from her lofty room, her heart
in turmoil, torn . . . should she keep her distance,
probe her husband? Or rush up to the man at once
and kiss his head and cling to both his hands?
As soon as she stepped across the stone threshold,
slipping in, she took a seat at the closest wall
and radiant in the firelight, faced Odysseus now.
There he sat, leaning against the great central column,
eyes fixed on the ground, waiting, poised for whatever
    words
his hardy wife might say when she caught sight of him.
A long while she sat in silence . . . numbing wonder
filled her heart as her eyes explored his face.
One moment he seemed . . . Odysseus, to the life –

the next, no, he was not the man she knew,
a huddled mass of rags was all she saw.

'Oh mother,' Telemachus reproached her,
'cruel mother, you with your hard heart!
Why do you spurn my father so – why don't you
sit beside him, engage him, ask him questions?
What other wife could have a spirit so unbending?
Holding back from her husband, home at last for *her*
after bearing twenty years of brutal struggle –
your heart was always harder than a rock!'

                      'My child,'
Penelope, well-aware, explained, 'I'm stunned with wonder,
powerless. Cannot speak to him, ask him questions,
look him in the eyes . . . But if he is truly
Odysseus, home at last, make no mistake:
we two will know each other, even better –
we two have secret signs,
known to us both but hidden from the world.'

Odysseus, long-enduring, broke into a smile
and turned to his son with pointed, winging words:
'Leave your mother here in the hall to test me
as she will. She soon will know me better.
Now because I am filthy, wear such grimy rags,
she spurns me – your mother still can't bring herself
to believe I am her husband.

                      But you and I,
put heads together. What's our best defense?
When someone kills a lone man in the realm
who leaves behind him no great band of avengers,

still the killer flees, goodbye to kin and country.
But *we* brought down the best of the island's princes,
the pillars of Ithaca. Weigh it well, I urge you.'

'Look to it all yourself now, father,' his son
deferred at once. 'You are the best on earth,
they say, when it comes to mapping tactics.
No one, no mortal man, can touch you there.
But we're behind you, hearts intent on battle,
nor do I think you'll find us short on courage,
long as our strength will last.'
                                                      'Then here's our plan,'
the master of tactics said. 'I think it's best.
First go and wash, and pull fresh tunics on
and tell the maids in the hall to dress well too.
And let the inspired bard take up his ringing lyre
and lead off for us all a dance so full of heart
that whoever hears the strains outside the gates –
a passerby on the road, a neighbor round about –
will think it's a wedding-feast that's under way.
No news of the suitors' death must spread through town
till we have slipped away to our own estates,
our orchard green with trees. There we'll see
what winning strategy Zeus will hand us then.'

They hung on his words and moved to orders smartly.
First they washed and pulled fresh tunics on,
the women arrayed themselves – the inspired bard
struck up his resounding lyre and stirred in all
a desire for dance and song, the lovely lilting beat,
till the great house echoed round to the measured tread

of dancing men in motion, women sashed and lithe.
And whoever heard the strains outside would say,
'A miracle – someone's married the queen at last!'

'One of her hundred suitors.'
                              'That callous woman,
too faithless to keep her lord and master's house
to the bitter end –'
                     'Till he came sailing home.'

So they'd say, blind to what had happened:
the great-hearted Odysseus was home again at last.
The maid Eurynome bathed him, rubbed him down with oil
and drew around him a royal cape and choice tunic too.
And Athena crowned the man with beauty, head to foot,
made him taller to all eyes, his build more massive,
yes, and down from his brow the great goddess
ran his curls like thick hyacinth clusters
full of blooms. As a master craftsman washes
gold over beaten silver – a man the god of fire
and Queen Athena trained in every fine technique –
and finishes off his latest effort, handsome work . . .
so she lavished splendor over his head and shoulders now.
He stepped from his bath, glistening like a god,
and back he went to the seat that he had left
and facing his wife, declared,
'Strange woman! So hard – the gods of Olympus
made you harder than any other woman in the world!
What other wife could have a spirit so unbending?
Holding back from her husband, home at last for *her*
after bearing twenty years of brutal struggle.

Come, nurse, make me a bed, I'll sleep alone.
She has a heart of iron in her breast.'

'Strange *man*,'
wary Penelope said. 'I'm not so proud, so scornful,
nor am I overwhelmed by your quick change . . .
You look – how well I know – the way he looked,
setting sail from Ithaca years ago
aboard the long-oared ship.

Come, Eurycleia,
move the sturdy bedstead out of our bridal chamber –
that room the master built with his own hands.
Take it out now, sturdy bed that it is,
and spread it deep with fleece,
blankets and lustrous throws to keep him warm.'

Putting her husband to the proof – but Odysseus
blazed up in fury, lashing out at his loyal wife:
'Woman – your words, they cut me to the core!
Who could move my bed? Impossible task,
even for some skilled craftsman – unless a god
came down in person, quick to lend a hand,
lifted it out with ease and moved it elsewhere.
Not a man on earth, not even at peak strength,
would find it easy to prise it up and shift it, no,
a great sign, a hallmark lies in its construction.
I know, I built it myself – no one else . . .
There was a branching olive-tree inside our court,
grown to its full prime, the bole like a column, thickset.
Around it I built my bedroom, finished off the walls
with good tight stonework, roofed it over soundly
and added doors, hung well and snugly wedged.

Then I lopped the leafy crown of the olive,
clean-cutting the stump bare from roots up,
planing it round with a bronze smoothing-adze –
I had the skill – I shaped it plumb to the line to make
my bedpost, bored the holes it needed with an auger.
Working from there I built my bed, start to finish,
I gave it ivory inlays, gold and silver fittings,
wove the straps across it, oxhide gleaming red.
There's our secret sign, I tell you, our life story!
Does the bed, my lady, still stand planted firm? –
I don't know – or has someone chopped away
that olive-trunk and hauled our bedstead off?'

                                               Living proof –
Penelope felt her knees go slack, her heart surrender,
recognizing the strong clear signs Odysseus offered.
She dissolved in tears, rushed to Odysseus, flung her arms
around his neck and kissed his head and cried out,
'Odysseus – don't flare up at me now, not you,
always the most understanding man alive!
The gods, it was the gods who sent us sorrow –
they grudged us both a life in each other's arms
from the heady zest of youth to the stoop of old age.
But don't fault me, angry with me now because I failed,
at the first glimpse, to greet you, hold you, so . . .
In my heart of hearts I always cringed with fear
some fraud might come, beguile me with his talk;
the world is full of the sort,
cunning ones who plot their own dark ends.
Remember Helen of Argos, Zeus's daughter –
would *she* have sported so in a stranger's bed
if she had dreamed that Achaea's sons were doomed

to fight and die to bring her home again?
Some god spurred her to do her shameless work.
Not till then did her mind conceive that madness,
blinding madness that caused her anguish, ours as well.
But now, since you have revealed such overwhelming proof –
the secret sign of our bed, which no one's ever seen
but you and I and a single handmaid, Actoris,
the servant my father gave me when I came,
who kept the doors of our room you built so well . . .
you've conquered my heart, my hard heart, at last!'

The more she spoke, the more a deep desire for tears
welled up inside his breast – he wept as he held the wife
he loved, the soul of loyalty, in his arms at last.
Joy, warm as the joy that shipwrecked sailors feel
when they catch sight of land – Poseidon has struck
their well-rigged ship on the open sea with gale winds
and crushing walls of waves, and only a few escape,
      swimming,
struggling out of the frothing surf to reach the shore,
their bodies crusted with salt but buoyed up with joy
as they plant their feet on solid ground again,
spared a deadly fate. So joyous now to her
the sight of her husband, vivid in her gaze,
that her white arms, embracing his neck
would never for a moment let him go . . .
Dawn with her rose-red fingers might have shone
upon their tears, if with her glinting eyes
Athena had not thought of one more thing.
She held back the night, and night lingered long
at the western edge of the earth, while in the east

she reined in Dawn of the golden throne at Ocean's banks,
commanding her not to yoke the windswift team that brings
   men light,
Blaze and Aurora, the young colts that race the Morning on.
Yet now Odysseus, seasoned veteran, said to his wife,
'Dear woman . . . we have still not reached the end
of all our trials. One more labor lies in store –
boundless, laden with danger, great and long,
and I must brave it out from start to finish.
So the ghost of Tiresias prophesied to me,
the day that I went down to the House of Death
to learn our best route home, my comrades' and my own.
But come, let's go to bed, dear woman – at long last
delight in sleep, delight in each other, come!'

   'If it's bed you want,' reserved Penelope replied,
'it's bed you'll have, whenever the spirit moves you,
now that the gods have brought you home again
to native land, your grand and gracious house.
But since you've alluded to it,
since a god has put it in your mind,
please, tell me about this trial still to come.
I'm bound to learn of it later, I am sure –
what's the harm if I hear of it tonight?'

                           'Still so strange,'
Odysseus, the old master of stories, answered.
'Why again, why force me to tell you all?
Well, tell I shall. I'll hide nothing now.
But little joy it will bring you, I'm afraid,
as little joy for me.

          The prophet said

that I must rove through towns on towns of men,
that I must carry a well-planed oar until
I come to a people who know nothing of the sea,
whose food is never seasoned with salt, strangers all
to ships with their crimson prows and long slim oars,
wings that make ships fly. And here is my sign,
he told me, clear, so clear I cannot miss it,
and I will share it with you now . . .
When another traveler falls in with me and calls
that weight across my shoulder a fan to winnow grain,
then, he told me, I must plant my oar in the earth
and sacrifice fine beasts to the lord god of the sea,
Poseidon – a ram, a bull and a ramping wild boar –
then journey home and render noble offerings up
to the deathless gods who rule the vaulting skies,
to all the gods in order.
And at last my own death will steal upon me . . .
a gentle, painless death, far from the sea it comes
to take me down, borne down with the years in ripe old age
with all my people here in blessed peace around me.
All this, the prophet said, will come to pass.'

'And so,' Penelope said, in her great wisdom,
'if the gods will really grant a happier old age,
there's hope that we'll escape our trials at last.'

So husband and wife confided in each other,
while nurse and Eurynome, under the flaring brands,
were making up the bed with coverings deep and soft.
And working briskly, soon as they'd made it snug,
back to her room the old nurse went to sleep

as Eurynome, their attendant, torch in hand,
lighted the royal couple's way to bed and,
leading them to their chamber, slipped away.
Rejoicing in each other, they returned to their bed,
the old familiar place they loved so well.

Now Telemachus, the cowherd and the swineherd
rested their dancing feet and had the women do the same,
and across the shadowed hall the men lay down to sleep.

But the royal couple, once they'd reveled in all
the longed-for joys of love, reveled in each other's stories,
the radiant woman telling of all she'd borne at home,
watching them there, the infernal crowd of suitors
slaughtering herds of cattle and good fat sheep –
while keen to win her hand –
draining the broached vats dry of vintage wine.
And great Odysseus told his wife of all the pains
he had dealt out to other men and all the hardships
he'd endured himself – his story first to last –
and she listened on, enchanted . . .
Sleep never sealed her eyes till all was told.

He launched in with how he fought the Cicones down,
then how he came to the Lotus-eaters' lush green land.
Then all the crimes of the Cyclops and how he paid him back
for the gallant men the monster ate without a qualm –
then how he visited Aeolus, who gave him a hero's welcome
then he sent him off, but the homeward run was not his fate,
not yet – some sudden squalls snatched him away once more
and drove him over the swarming sea, groaning in despair.

Then how he moored at Telepylus, where Laestrygonians
wrecked his fleet and killed his men-at-arms.
He told her of Circe's cunning magic wiles
and how he voyaged down in his long benched ship
to the moldering House of Death, to consult Tiresias,
ghostly seer of Thebes, and he saw old comrades there
and he saw his mother, who bore and reared him as a child.
He told how he caught the Sirens' voices throbbing in the wind
and how he had scudded past the Clashing Rocks, past grim
    Charybdis,
past Scylla – whom no rover had ever coasted by, home free –
and how his shipmates slaughtered the cattle of the Sun
and Zeus the king of thunder split his racing ship
with a reeking bolt and killed his hardy comrades,
all his fighting men at a stroke, but he alone
escaped their death at sea. He told how he reached
Ogygia's shores and the nymph Calypso held him back,
deep in her arching caverns, craving him for a husband –
cherished him, vowed to make him immortal, ageless, all his
    days,
yes, but she never won the heart inside him, never . . .
then how he reached the Phaeacians – heavy sailing there –
who with all their hearts had prized him like a god
and sent him off in a ship to his own beloved land,
giving him bronze and hoards of gold and robes . . .
and that was the last he told her, just as sleep
overcame him . . . sleep loosing his limbs,
slipping the toils of anguish from his mind.

Athena, her eyes afire, had fresh plans.
Once she thought he'd had his heart's content

of love and sleep at his wife's side, straightaway
she roused young Dawn from Ocean's banks to her golden
    throne
to bring men light and roused Odysseus too, who rose
from his soft bed and advised his wife in parting,
'Dear woman, we both have had our fill of trials.
You in our house, weeping over my journey home,
fraught with storms and torment, true, and I,
pinned down in pain by Zeus and other gods,
for all my desire, blocked from reaching home.
But now that we've arrived at our bed together –
the reunion that we yearned for all those years –
look after the things still left me in our house.
But as for the flocks those brazen suitors plundered,
much I'll recoup myself, making many raids;
the rest our fellow-Ithacans will supply
till all my folds are full of sheep again.
But now I must be off to the upland farm,
our orchard green with trees, to see my father,
good old man weighed down with so much grief for me.
And you, dear woman, sensible as you are,
I would advise you, still . . .
quick as the rising sun the news will spread
of the suitors that I killed inside the house.
So climb to your lofty chamber with your women.
Sit tight there. See no one. Question no one.'

He strapped his burnished armor round his shoulders,
roused Telemachus, the cowherd and the swineherd,
and told them to take up weapons honed for battle.
They snapped to commands, harnessed up in bronze,

opened the doors and strode out, Odysseus in the lead.
By now the daylight covered the land, but Pallas,
shrouding them all in darkness,
quickly led the four men out of town.

7

Peace

Now Cyllenian Hermes called away the suitors' ghosts,
holding firm in his hand the wand of fine pure gold
that enchants the eyes of men whenever Hermes wants
or wakes us up from sleep.
With a wave of this he stirred and led them on
and the ghosts trailed after with high thin cries
as bats cry in the depths of a dark haunted cavern,
shrilling, flittering, wild when one drops from the chain –
slipped from the rock face, while the rest cling tight . . .
So with their high thin cries the ghosts flocked now
and Hermes the Healer led them on, and down the dank
moldering paths and past the Ocean's streams they went
and past the White Rock and the Sun's Western Gates and
        past
the Land of Dreams, and they soon reached the fields of
        asphodel
where the dead, the burnt-out wraiths of mortals, make their
        home.

  There they found the ghosts of Peleus' son Achilles,
Patroclus, fearless Antilochus – and Great Ajax too,
the first in stature, first in build and bearing
of all the Argives after Peleus' matchless son.
They had grouped around Achilles' ghost, and now
the shade of Atreus' son Agamemnon marched toward them –

fraught with grief and flanked by all his comrades,
troops of his men-at-arms who died beside him,
who met their fate in lord Aegisthus' halls.
Achilles' ghost was first to greet him: 'Agamemnon,
you were the one, we thought, of all our fighting princes
Zeus who loves the lightning favored most, all your days,
because you commanded such a powerful host of men
on the fields of Troy where we Achaeans suffered.
But you were doomed to encounter fate so early,
you too, yet no one born escapes its deadly force.
If only you had died your death in the full flush
of the glory you had mastered – died on Trojan soil!
Then all united Achaea would have raised your tomb
and you'd have won your son great fame for years to come.
Not so. You were fated to die a wretched death.'

    And the ghost of Atrides Agamemnon answered,
'Son of Peleus, great godlike Achilles! Happy man,
you died on the fields of Troy, a world away from home,
and the best of Trojan and Argive champions died around
        you,
fighting for your corpse. And you . . . there you lay
in the whirling dust, overpowered in all your power
and wiped from memory all your horseman's skills.
That whole day we fought, we'd never have stopped
if Zeus had not stopped *us* with sudden gales.
Then we bore you out of the fighting, onto the ships,
we laid you down on a litter, cleansed your handsome flesh
with warm water and soothing oils, and round your body
troops of Danaans wept hot tears and cut their locks.
Hearing the news, your mother, Thetis, rose from the sea,

immortal sea-nymphs in her wake, and a strange unearthly
    cry
came throbbing over the ocean. Terror gripped Achaea's
    armies,
they would have leapt in panic, boarded the long hollow ships
if one man, deep in his age-old wisdom, had not checked
    them:
Nestor – from the first his counsel always seemed the best,
and now, concerned for the ranks, he rose and shouted,
"Hold fast, Argives! Sons of Achaea, don't run now!
This is Achilles' mother rising from the sea
with all her immortal sea-nymphs –
she longs to join her son who died in battle!"
That stopped our panicked forces in their tracks
as the Old Man of the Sea's daughters gathered round you –
wailing, heartsick – dressed you in ambrosial, deathless robes
and the Muses, nine in all, voice-to-voice in choirs,
their vibrant music rising, raised your dirge.
Not one soldier would you have seen dry-eyed,
the Muses' song so pierced us to the heart.
For seventeen days unbroken, days and nights
we mourned you – immortal gods and mortal men.
At the eighteenth dawn we gave you to the flames
and slaughtered around your body droves of fat sheep
and shambling longhorn cattle, and you were burned
in the garments of the gods and laved with soothing oils
and honey running sweet, and a long cortege of Argive
    heroes
paraded in review, in battle armor round your blazing pyre,
men in chariots, men on foot – a resounding roar went up.
And once the god of fire had burned your corpse to ash,

at first light we gathered your white bones, Achilles,
cured them in strong neat wine and seasoned oils.
Your mother gave us a gold two-handled urn,
a gift from Dionysus, she said,
a masterwork of the famous Smith, the god of fire.
Your white bones rest in that, my brilliant Achilles,
mixed with the bones of dead Patroclus, Menoetius' son,
apart from those of Antilochus, whom you treasured
more than all other comrades once Patroclus died.
Over your bones we reared a grand, noble tomb –
devoted veterans all, Achaea's combat forces –
high on its jutting headland over the Hellespont's
broad reach, a landmark glimpsed from far out at sea
by men of our own day and men of days to come.

                          And then
your mother, begging the gods for priceless trophies,
set them out in the ring for all our champions.
You in your day have witnessed funeral games
for many heroes, games to honor the death of kings,
when young men cinch their belts, tense to win some prize –
but if you'd laid eyes on these it would have thrilled your
    heart,
magnificent trophies the goddess, glistening-footed Thetis,
held out in your honor. You were dear to the gods,
so even in death your name will never die . . .
Great glory is yours, Achilles,
for all time, in the eyes of all mankind!

                           But I?
What joy for *me* when the coil of war had wound down?
For my return Zeus hatched a pitiful death
at the hands of Aegisthus – and my accursed wife.'

As they exchanged the stories of their fates,
Hermes the guide and giant-killer drew up close to both,
leading down the ghosts of the suitors King Odysseus killed.
Struck by the sight, the two went up to them right away
and the ghost of Atreus' son Agamemnon recognized
the noted prince Amphimedon, Melaneus' dear son
who received him once in Ithaca, at his home,
and Atrides' ghost called out to his old friend now,
'Amphimedon, what disaster brings you down to the dark
    world?
All of you, good picked men, and all in your prime –
no captain out to recruit the best in any city
could have chosen better. What laid you low?
Wrecked in the ships when lord Poseidon roused
same punishing blast of gales and heavy breakers?
Or did ranks of enemies mow you down on land
as you tried to raid and cut off herds and flocks
or fought to win their city, take their women?
Answer me, tell me. I was once your guest.
Don't you recall the day I came to visit
your house in Ithaca – King Menelaus came too –
to urge Odysseus to sail with us in the ships
on our campaign to Troy? And the long slow voyage,
crossing wastes of ocean, cost us one whole month.
That's how hard it was to bring him round,
Odysseus, raider of cities.'

                      'Famous Atrides!'
Amphimedon's ghost called back. 'Lord of men,
    Agamemnon,
I remember it all, your majesty, as you say,
and I will tell you, start to finish now,

the story of our death,
the brutal end contrived to take us off.
We were courting the wife of Odysseus, gone so long.
She neither spurned nor embraced a marriage she despised,
no, she simply planned our death, our black doom!
This was her latest masterpiece of guile:
she set up a great loom in the royal halls
and she began to weave, and the weaving finespun,
the yarns endless, and she would lead us on: 'Young men,
my suitors, now that King Odysseus is no more,
go slowly, keen as you are to marry me, until
I can finish off this web . . .
so my weaving won't all fray and come to nothing.
This is a shroud for old lord Laertes, for that day
when the deadly fate that lays us out at last will take him
    down.
I dread the shame my countrywomen would heap upon me,
yes, if a man of such wealth should lie in state
without a shroud for cover.'
                Her very words,
and despite our pride and passion we believed her.
So by day she'd weave at her great and growing web –
by night, by the light of torches set beside her,
she would unravel all she'd done. Three whole years
she deceived us blind, seduced us with this scheme . . .
Then, when the wheeling seasons brought the fourth year
    on
and the months waned and the long days came round once
    more,
one of her women, in on the queen's secret, told the truth
and we caught her in the act – unweaving her gorgeous web.

So she finished it off. Against her will. We forced her.
But just as she bound off that great shroud and washed it,
spread it out – glistening like the sunlight or the moon –
just then some wicked spirit brought Odysseus back,
from god knows where, to the edge of his estate
where the swineherd kept his pigs. And back too,
to the same place, came Odysseus' own dear son,
scudding home in his black ship from sandy Pylos.
The pair of them schemed our doom, our deathtrap,
then lit out for town –
Telemachus first in fact, Odysseus followed,
later, led by the swineherd, and clad in tatters,
looking for all the world like an old and broken beggar
hunched on a stick, his body wrapped in shameful rags.
Disguised so none of us, not even the older ones,
could spot that tramp for the man he really was,
bursting in on us there, out of the blue. No,
we attacked him, blows and insults flying fast,
and he took it all for a time, in his own house,
all the taunts and blows – he had a heart of iron.
But once the will of thundering Zeus had roused his blood,
he and Telemachus bore the burnished weapons off
and stowed them deep in a storeroom, shot the bolts
and he – the soul of cunning – told his wife to set
the great bow and the gleaming iron axes out
before the suitors – all of us doomed now –
to test our skill and bring our slaughter on . . .
Not one of us had the strength to string that powerful
      weapon,
all of us fell far short of what it took. But then,
when the bow was coming round to Odysseus' hands,

we raised a hue and cry – he must not have it,
no matter how he begged! Only Telemachus
urged him to take it up, and once he got it
in his clutches, long-suffering great Odysseus
strung his bow with ease and shot through all the axes,
then, vaulting onto the threshold, stood there poised, and
    pouring
his flashing arrows out before him, glaring for the kill,
he cut Antinous down, then shot his painful arrows
into the rest of us, aiming straight and true,
and down we went, corpse on corpse in droves.
Clearly a god was driving him and all his henchmen,
routing us headlong in their fury down the hall,
wheeling into the slaughter, slashing left and right
and grisly screams broke from skulls cracked open –
the whole floor awash with blood.

               So we died,
Agamemnon . . . our bodies lie untended even now,
strewn in Odysseus' palace. They know nothing yet,
the kin in our houses who might wash our wounds
of clotted gore and lay us out and mourn us.
These are the solemn honors owed the dead.'

                     'Happy Odysseus!'
Agamemnon's ghost cried out. 'Son of old Laertes –
mastermind – what a fine, faithful wife you won!
What good sense resided in your Penelope –
how well Icarius' daughter remembered you,
Odysseus, the man she married once!
The fame of her great virtue will never die.
The immortal gods will lift a song for all mankind,
a glorious song in praise of self-possessed Penelope.

A far cry from the daughter of Tyndareus, Clytemnestra –
what outrage she committed, killing the man *she* married
    once! –
yes, and the song men sing of her will ring with loathing.
She brands with a foul name the breed of womankind,
even the honest ones to come!'
                        So they traded stories,
the two ghosts standing there in the House of Death,
far in the hidden depths below the earth.

   Odysseus and his men had stridden down from town
and quickly reached Laertes' large, well-tended farm
that the old king himself had wrested from the wilds,
years ago, laboring long and hard. His lodge was here
and around it stretched a row of sheds where fieldhands,
bondsmen who did his bidding, sat and ate and slept.
And an old Sicilian woman was in charge,
who faithfully looked after her aged master
out on his good estate remote from town.
Odysseus told his servants and his son,
'Into the timbered lodge now, go, quickly,
kill us the fattest porker, fix our meal.
And I will put my father to the test,
see if the old man knows me now, on sight,
or fails to, after twenty years apart.'

   With that he passed his armor to his men
and in they went at once, his son as well. Odysseus
wandered off, approaching the thriving vineyard, searching,
picking his way down to the great orchard, searching,
but found neither Dolius nor his sons nor any hand.

They'd just gone off, old Dolius in the lead,
to gather stones for a dry retaining wall
to shore the vineyard up. But he did find
his father, alone, on that well-worked plot,
spading round a sapling – clad in filthy rags,
in a patched, unseemly shirt, and round his shins
he had some oxhide leggings strapped, patched too,
to keep from getting scraped, and gloves on his hands
to fight against the thorns, and on his head
he wore a goatskin skullcap
to cultivate his misery that much more . . .
Long-enduring Odysseus, catching sight of him now –
a man worn down with years, his heart racked with sorrow –
halted under a branching pear-tree, paused and wept.
Debating, head and heart, what should he do now?
Kiss and embrace his father, pour out the long tale –
now he had made the journey home to native land –
or probe him first and test him every way?
Torn, mulling it over, this seemed better:
test the old man first,
reproach him with words that cut him to the core.
Convinced, Odysseus went right up to his father.
Laertes was digging round the sapling, head bent low
as his famous offspring hovered over him and began,
'You want no skill, old man, at tending a garden.
All's well-kept here; not one thing in the plot,
no plant, no fig, no pear, no olive, no vine,
not a vegetable, lacks your tender, loving care.
But I must say – and don't be offended now –
your plants are doing better than yourself.
Enough to be stooped with age

but look how squalid you are, those shabby rags.
Surely it's not for sloth your master lets you go to seed.
There's nothing of slave about your build or bearing.
I have eyes: you look like a king to me. The sort
entitled to bathe, sup well, then sleep in a soft bed.
That's the right and pride of you old-timers.
Come now, tell me – in no uncertain terms –
whose slave are you? whose orchard are you tending?
And tell me this – I must be absolutely sure –
this place I've reached, is it truly Ithaca?
Just as that fellow told me, just now . . .
I fell in with him on the road here. Clumsy,
none too friendly, couldn't trouble himself
to hear me out or give me a decent answer
when I asked about a long-lost friend of mine,
whether he's still alive, somewhere in Ithaca,
or dead and gone already, lost in the House of Death.
Do you want to hear his story? Listen. Catch my drift.
I once played host to a man in my own country;
he'd come to my door, the most welcome guest
from foreign parts I ever entertained.
He claimed he came of good Ithacan stock,
said his father was Arcesius' son, Laertes.
So I took the new arrival under my own roof,
I gave him a hero's welcome, treated him in style –
stores in our palace made for princely entertainment.
And I gave my friend some gifts to fit his station,
handed him seven bars of well-wrought gold,
a mixing-bowl of solid silver, etched with flowers,
a dozen cloaks, unlined and light, a dozen rugs
and as many full-cut capes and shirts as well,

and to top it off, four women, perfect beauties
skilled in crafts – he could pick them out himself.'

   'Stranger,' his father answered, weeping softly,
'the land you've reached is the very one you're after,
true, but it's in the grip of reckless, lawless men.
And as for the gifts you showered on your guest,
you gave them all for nothing.
But if you'd found him alive, here in Ithaca,
he would have replied in kind, with gift for gift,
and entertained you warmly before he sent you off.
That's the old custom, when one has led the way.
But tell me, please – in no uncertain terms –
how many years ago did you host the man,
that unfortunate guest of yours, my son . . .
there was a son, or was he all a dream?
That most unlucky man, whom now, I fear,
far from his own soil and those he loves,
the fish have swallowed down on the high seas
or birds and beasts on land have made their meal.
Nor could the ones who bore him – mother, father –
wrap his corpse in a shroud and mourn him deeply.
Nor could his warm, generous wife, so self-possessed,
Penelope, ever keen for her husband on his deathbed,
the fit and proper way, or close his eyes at last.
These are the solemn honors owed the dead.
But tell me your own story – that I'd like to know:
Who are you? where are you from? your city? your parents?
Where does the ship lie moored that brought you here,
your hardy shipmates too? Or did you arrive
as a passenger aboard some stranger's craft

and men who put you ashore have pulled away?'

           'The whole tale,'
his crafty son replied, 'I'll tell you start to finish.
I come from Roamer-Town, my home's a famous place,
my father's Unsparing, son of old King Pain,
and my name's Man of Strife . . .
I sailed from Sicily, aye, but some ill wind
blew me here, off course – much against my will –
and my ship lies moored off farmlands far from town.
As for Odysseus, well, five years have passed
since he left my house and put my land behind him,
luckless man! But the birds were good as he launched out,
all on the right, and I rejoiced as I sent him off
and he rejoiced in sailing. We had high hopes
we'd meet again as guests, as old friends,
and trade some shining gifts.'

         At those words
a black cloud of grief came shrouding over Laertes.
Both hands clawing the ground for dirt and grime,
he poured it over his grizzled head, sobbing, in spasms.
Odysseus' heart shuddered, a sudden twinge went shooting
  up
through his nostrils, watching his dear father struggle . . .
He sprang toward him, kissed him, hugged him, crying,
'Father – I am your son – myself, the man you're seeking,
home after twenty years, on native ground at last!
Hold back your tears, your grief.
Let me tell you the news, but we must hurry –
I've cut the suitors down in our own house,
I've paid them back their outrage, vicious crimes!'

           'Odysseus . . .'

Laertes, catching his breath, found words to answer.
'You – you're truly my son, Odysseus, home at last?
Give me a sign, some proof – I must be sure.'

                                    'This scar first,'
quick to the mark, his son said, 'look at this –
the wound I took from the boar's white tusk
on Mount Parnassus. There you'd sent me, you
and mother, to see her fond old father, Autolycus,
and collect the gifts he vowed to give me, once,
when he came to see us here.

                            Or these, these trees –
let me tell you the trees you gave me years ago,
here on this well-worked plot . . .
I begged you for everything I saw, a little boy
trailing you through the orchard, picking our way
among these trees, and you named them one by one.
You gave me thirteen pear, ten apple trees
and forty figs – and promised to give me, look,
fifty vinerows, bearing hard on each other's heels,
clusters of grapes year-round at every grade of ripeness,
mellowed as Zeus's seasons weigh them down.'

                                  Living proof –
and Laertes' knees went slack, his heart surrendered,
recognizing the strong clear signs Odysseus offered.
He threw his arms around his own dear son, fainting
as hardy great Odysseus hugged him to his heart
until he regained his breath, came back to life
and cried out, 'Father Zeus –
you gods of Olympus, you still rule on high
if those suitors have truly paid in blood
for all their reckless outrage! Oh, but now

my heart quakes with fear that all the Ithacans
will come down on us in a pack, at any time,
and rush the alarm through every island town!'

'There's nothing to fear,' his canny son replied,
'put it from your mind. Let's make for your lodge
beside the orchard here. I sent Telemachus on ahead,
the cowherd, swineherd too, to fix a hasty meal.'

So the two went home, confiding all the way
and arriving at the ample, timbered lodge,
they found Telemachus with the two herdsmen
carving sides of meat and mixing ruddy wine.
Before they ate, the Sicilian serving-woman
bathed her master, Laertes – his spirits high
in his own room – and rubbed him down with oil
and round his shoulders drew a fresh new cloak.
And Athena stood beside him, fleshing out the limbs
of the old commander, made him taller to all eyes,
his build more massive, stepping from his bath,
so his own son gazed at him, wonderstruck –
face-to-face he seemed a deathless god . . .
'Father' – Odysseus' words had wings – 'surely
one of the everlasting gods has made you
taller, stronger, shining in my eyes!'

Facing his son, the wise old man returned,
'If only – Father Zeus, Athena and lord Apollo –
I were the man I was, king of the Cephallenians
when I sacked the city of Nericus, sturdy fortress
out on its jutting cape! If I'd been young in arms

last night in our house with harness on my back,
standing beside you, fighting off the suitors,
how many I would have cut the knees from under –
the heart inside you would have leapt for joy!'

   So father and son confirmed each other's spirits.
And then, with the roasting done, the meal set out,
the others took their seats on chairs and stools,
were just putting their hands to bread and meat
when old Dolius trudged in with his sons,
worn out from the fieldwork.
The old Sicilian had gone and fetched them home,
the mother who reared the boys and tended Dolius well,
now that the years had ground the old man down . . .
When they saw Odysseus – knew him in their bones –
they stopped in their tracks, staring, struck dumb,
but the king waved them on with a warm and easy air:
'Sit down to your food, old friend. Snap out of your
      wonder.
We've been cooling our heels here long enough,
eager to get our hands on all this pork,
hoping you'd all troop in at any moment.'

   Spreading his arms, Dolius rushed up to him,
clutched Odysseus by the wrist and kissed his hand,
greeting his king now with a burst of winging words:
'Dear master, you're back – the answer to our prayers!
We'd lost all hope but the gods have brought you home!
Welcome – health! The skies rain blessings on you!
But tell me the truth now – this I'd like to know –
shrewd Penelope, has she heard you're home?

Or should we send a messenger?'
                                              'She knows by now,
old man,' his wily master answered brusquely.
'Why busy yourself with that?'

   So Dolius went back to his sanded stool.
His sons too, pressing around the famous king,
greeted Odysseus warmly, grasped him by the hand
then took their seats in order by their father.

   But now, as they fell to supper in the lodge,
Rumor the herald sped like wildfire through the city,
crying out the news of the suitors' bloody death and doom,
and massing from every quarter as they listened, kinsmen
   milled
with wails and moans of grief before Odysseus' palace.
And then they carried out the bodies, every family
buried their own, and the dead from other towns
they loaded onto the rapid ships for crews
to ferry back again, each to his own home . . .
Then in a long, mourning file they moved to assembly
where, once they'd grouped, crowding the meeting grounds,
old lord Eupithes rose in their midst to speak out.
Unforgettable sorrow wrung his heart for his son,
Antinous, the first that great Odysseus killed.
In tears for the one he lost, he stood and cried,
'My friends, what a mortal blow this man has dealt
to all our island people! Those fighters, many and brave,
he led away in his curved ships – he lost the ships
and he lost the men and back he comes again
to kill the best of our Cephallenian princes.

Quick, after him! Before he flees to Pylos
or holy Elis, where Epeans rule in power –
up, attack! Or we'll hang our heads forever,
all disgraced, even by generations down the years,
if we don't punish the murderers of our brothers and our
    sons!
Why, life would lose its relish – for me, at least –
I'd rather die at once and go among the dead.
Attack! – before the assassins cross the sea
and leave us in their wake.'

                        He closed in tears
and compassion ran through every Achaean there.
Suddenly Medon and the inspired bard approached them,
fresh from Odysseus' house, where they had just awakened.
They strode into the crowds; amazement took each man
but the herald Medon spoke in all his wisdom:
'Hear me, men of Ithaca. Not without the hand
of the deathless gods did Odysseus do these things!
Myself, I saw an immortal fighting at his side –
like Mentor to the life. I saw the same god,
now in front of Odysseus, spurring him on,
now stampeding the suitors through the hall,
crazed with fear, and down they went in droves!'

   Terror gripped them all, their faces ashen white.
At last the old warrior Halitherses, Mastor's son –
who alone could see the days behind and days ahead –
rose up and spoke, distraught for each man there:
'Hear me, men of Ithaca. Hear what I have to say.
Thanks to your own craven hearts these things were done!
You never listened to me or the good commander Mentor,

you never put a stop to your sons' senseless folly.
What fine work they did, so blind, so reckless,
carving away the wealth, affronting the wife
of a great and famous man, telling themselves
that he'd return no more! So let things rest now.
Listen to me for once – I say don't attack!
Else some will draw the lightning on their necks.'

So he urged
and some held fast to their seats, but more than half
sprang up with warcries now. They had no taste
for the prophet's sane plan – winning Eupithes
quickly won them over. They ran for armor
and once they'd harnessed up in burnished bronze
they grouped in ranks before the terraced city.
Eupithes led them on in their foolish, mad campaign,
certain he would avenge the slaughter of his son
but the father was not destined to return –
he'd meet his death in battle then and there.

  Athena at this point made appeals to Zeus:
'Father, son of Cronus, our high and mighty king,
now let me ask you a question . . .
tell me the secrets hidden in your mind.
Will you prolong the pain, the cruel fighting here
or hand down pacts of peace between both sides?'

  'My child,' Zeus who marshals the thunderheads replied,
'why do you pry and probe me so intently? Come now,
wasn't the plan your own? You conceived it yourself:
Odysseus should return and pay the traitors back.
Do as your heart desires –

but let me tell you how it should be done.
Now that royal Odysseus has taken his revenge,
let both sides seal their pacts that he shall reign for life,
and let us purge their memories of the bloody slaughter
of their brothers and their sons. Let them be friends,
devoted as in the old days. Let peace and wealth
come cresting through the land.'

                    So Zeus decreed
and launched Athena already poised for action –
down she swept from Olympus' craggy peaks.

  By then Odysseus' men had had their fill
of hearty fare, and the seasoned captain said,
'One of you go outside – see if they're closing in.'
A son of Dolius snapped to his command,
ran to the door and saw them all too close
and shouted back to Odysseus,
'They're on top of us! To arms – and fast!'
Up they sprang and strapped themselves in armor,
the three men with Odysseus, Dolius' six sons
and Dolius and Laertes clapped on armor too,
gray as they were, but they would fight if forced.
Once they had all harnessed up in burnished bronze
they opened the doors and strode out, Odysseus in the lead.

  And now, taking the build and voice of Mentor,
Zeus's daughter Athena marched right in.
The good soldier Odysseus thrilled to see her,
turned to his son and said in haste, 'Telemachus,
you'll learn soon enough – as you move up to fight
where champions strive to prove themselves the best –

not to disgrace your father's line a moment.
In battle prowess we've excelled for ages
all across the world.'
                    Telemachus reassured him,
'Now you'll see, if you care to watch, father,
now I'm fired up. Disgrace, you say?
I won't disgrace your line!'

   Laertes called out in deep delight,
'What a day for me, dear gods! What joy –
my son and my grandson vying over courage!'
                                'Laertes!'
Goddess Athena rushed beside him, eyes ablaze:
'Son of Arcesius, dearest of all my comrades,
say a prayer to the bright-eyed girl and Father Zeus,
then brandish your long spear and wing it fast!'

   Athena breathed enormous strength in the old man.
He lifted a prayer to mighty Zeus's daughter,
brandished his spear a moment, winged it fast
and hit Eupithes, pierced his bronze-sided helmet
that failed to block the bronze point tearing through –
down Eupithes crashed, his armor clanging against his chest.
Odysseus and his gallant son charged straight at the front lines,
slashing away with swords, with two-edged spears and now
they would have killed them all, cut them off from home
if Athena, daughter of storming Zeus, had not cried out
in a piercing voice that stopped all fighters cold,
'Hold back, you men of Ithaca, back from brutal war!
Break off – shed no more blood – make peace at once!'

So Athena commanded. Terror blanched their faces,
they went limp with fear, weapons slipped from their hands
and strewed the ground at the goddess' ringing voice.
They spun in flight to the city, wild to save their lives,
but loosing a savage cry, the long-enduring great Odysseus,
gathering all his force, swooped like a soaring eagle –
just as the son of Cronus hurled a reeking bolt
that fell at her feet, the mighty Father's daughter,
and blazing-eyed Athena wheeled on Odysseus, crying,
'Royal son of Laertes, Odysseus, master of exploits,
hold back now! Call a halt to the great leveler, War –
don't court the rage of Zeus who rules the world!'

So she commanded. He obeyed her, glad at heart.
And Athena handed down her pacts of peace
between both sides for all the years to come –
the daughter of Zeus whose shield is storm and thunder,
yes, but the goddess still kept Mentor's build and voice.

[. . .]